3

Uncertain Times

ISBN: 0-9856-6791-5
ISBN-13: 9780985667917

Uncertain Times
A Story of Survival
A Novel

Travis Wright
Edited by Hannah Heimbuch
Photographs by Logan Parks
Illustrated by Melanie Noblin

"All that is necessary for the triumph of evil is for good men to do nothing."

-Edmund Burke

Chapter One: Reflections
(The near Future)

It was a calm cool morning; with a slight breeze blowing out of the Northeast. It was a balmy three degrees above zero. The cold snap had dipped to thirty-five below and lasted for the better part of a month; it took its toll on both sides before it finally subsided. Men and women were lost to the extreme cold. The battle only lasted a week, but had to be stopped because of the freezing weather. Machines, weapons and men no longer worked. When the fighting started, no one knew the cold would cause just as many deaths as the bullets. The enemy had been beaten, but how badly? When would they be back? They didn't risk sending more men out to possibly lose them too. They had a secure perimeter for now and would let them make the next move.

The whole situation, being driven from home, the scarcity of food and water, the cold and lack of sleep and not knowing when you would be shot at next was enough to drive the strongest man insane.

Jim was on close perimeter security, half a click outside the cave with his FNH SCAR 17, heavy chambered in .308 caliber, which he had turned into a sniper rifle with a large power scope on it. The cave was a compound for the resistance based in the Timber Wolf Mountains of southcentral Alaska. One of the last groups in the area still fighting the world government led by the U.N.

"Morning, Sarge," whispered a lean young man not old enough to shave.

"How we doing son and why are you whispering?" His name was Todd and he was Jim's second oldest son.

"It's just so quiet out here. It doesn't feel right if I don't whisper."

"I know what you mean, son."

"We get a mission yet?" asked Todd, clutching his AK-47.

"The recon patrol got back at 3 a.m. and debriefed. They are getting some much needed sleep. We will have a new plan of attack soon," said Jim. "In the meantime, here is a list of men we will need tonight. Do me a favor and have little Matt round them up this morning, will ya?"

"I still think that guy is crazy," said Todd.

"He's not crazy, he's just a little extreme and right now that is exactly what we need. Just tell them to meet in the cabin at 1400."

"Dad, when am I going to get to go?" Todd asked, not seeing his name on the paper. "You've trained me well and I *am* old enough now."

"Not yet Todd, I want you to enjoy life after we've won our freedom back. I don't want to lose you; a father should never have to bury his son. Now off you go."

The boy was stubborn, but listened to reason. At seventeen, he was a tall and strong young man. He played football and had dreams of playing in the NFL. As team captain and quarterback, he could handle tough situations and read the plays well. He would make a great military leader, but not yet. He had grown up with a dad barking orders like he was a recruit, but it turned him into a fine young man.

Todd made his way back up through the perimeter and the craters made from the mortars and tank rounds from their friends down the mountain. As he walked up toward the cave, the occasional body part or complete corpse could be seen partly buried in the snow. He couldn't smell it because of the cold, but death was in the air.

It had been three long years of fighting since the first shots were fired. Jim remembered it all too well and was growing tired. *I'm just going to sit here a little longer,* he thought to himself. The loss of blood, sweat and tears, all of these things weighed heavily on his mind. Jim just kept telling himself and the others that all this would be worth it and things would get better. But, even he was starting to doubt his resolve.

"An armed man is a citizen, an unarmed man is a subject."

—*Anonymous*

Chapter Two: Just Like Any Other Day
(Present Day)

Just like every morning, Jim woke up and started the coffee. It was a bright and sunny morning in July, with a temperature of about 60 degrees. "Going to be another hot one, baby," Jim said to his wife Mary. "Going to town today?" Jim asked.

"With all the kids," groaned Mary. "I suppose we could use more groceries."

"Make this deposit for me, will you?"

"Sure," said Mary.

Jim took a shower and got dressed. Before he headed out to his gun store, *Jim's Guns, Ammo, and Tackle,* a few miles down the road, he had to visit his personal gun room. It was always a question in the morning of which handgun to carry, but he usually settled back to his trusty 1911 .45 ACP.

Cody, Jim's youngest boy, walked in.

"Do you need any help?" Cody asked.

"Not this morning, son." Jim was always recruiting the kids to help load ammo cans or the magazines to half full. He always made sure the magazines had something in them, so the springs would last.

"When can we go shooting again?" asked Cody.

"We'll go soon," said Jim. "We have some fishing to do and after that we can go to the range."

"Can I shoot my AK-47 again? I really liked that one last time."

"You sure can." Cody was only ten years old and scrawny, but he could shoot the AK pretty well. "I'll see you tonight. Now look out so I can lock up." Cody moved out of the way so his dad could lock up the gun room and go to work.

Jim opened up his gun store a few years after moving to Alaska. He met Mary soon after. With his experience with firearms, it was a perfect fit for him. Jim grew up hunting and fishing in a small town in Oregon that few had ever heard of. He remembered going blacktail deer hunting in his younger years with just a .22 rifle and open sights. As long as he either shot a deer or got home for supper he didn't get the belt. He and his friends would have shooting matches in the backyard to see who could shoot the worm in half or shoot the empty .22 shell off the block of wood. In Marine Corps boot camp, Jim received an expert badge during his shooting qualification and continued to receive them throughout his career.

Jim got into his truck and started down the road. "Not much traffic today," he said to himself as he reached for the radio knob. Something was strange about today, no traffic lights and the radio was all static. As Jim approached his store, he heard an alarm sounding.

"That better not be mine!" Jim said out loud.

Sure enough, it was and there were people in the store as well as people carrying things out. Jim sped up to get there faster. After coming to a stop outside the store, Jim pulled his 1911 .45 ACP from his holster and got out of his truck. "What the hell is going on here?" Jim yelled. The alarm was deafening. "All of you put that stuff down or I will open fire!" The people, realizing that Jim meant business, put all the guns, bulk ammo and other things back without a fight and the alarm was finally turned off.

"Now, will someone please tell me what the hell you are doing in my store?" Jim asked, pointing his .45 at them.

"Haven't you heard?" asked one of the thieves.

"Heard what?" asked Jim.

"The government gave up control of the military this morning and the United Nations has implemented martial law in the U.S."

"So," Jim said. "You figured you would just help yourself to my stuff since the world is coming to an end, is that it? Listen up everyone, if this is true then we are all in trouble, I say we find out all we can and then take action in an orderly fashion. Is local law enforcement on our side or theirs? When are troops coming here to Alaska, or are they already here? We need to find out everything we can. If you need something, I will sell it to you."

"Money isn't going to be worth anything to you if this is all true!" said one of the men in the store.

Jim knew he was right. Tensions had been rising worldwide for some time and U.N. troops were always the ones sent in to quell the violence, but why here? The United States wasn't one of those countries that troops got sent too because it was out of control. Everything was fine here. This was no longer about conspiracies, this was the point of no return.

"It's going to be business as usual until I get some kind of confirmation. Now all of you get out of here or buy something." Jim was well known and respected in the community. Just about everyone knew him and he couldn't go anywhere without someone wanting to talk guns. Jim and Mary belonged to many organizations and donated to worthy causes quite often. Jim didn't like all of the attention and would joke about the paparazzi and fans wanting his autograph. Just then, a truck dove into the parking lot, very fast. It was Danny.

He got out of his truck in front of the building and went running into the gun store. "Jim, Jim!" Danny was excited as usual. "Did you hear the news, Jim?" Danny asked.

"Yes, Danny. Now calm down. We need to find out as much information as we can. In the meantime, with the door broke we need to load the trucks with as much of this as we can. Got your gun on you?"

"You know it." Danny flashed his Glock .40 S&W to Jim. "Does anyone want to buy anything?" The people that were left just stared at Jim. "Ok then, get out if you're not buying."

"Are you going to make them pay for the door?" asked Danny.

"They're right, money won't be worth anything."

As Jim and Danny loaded the trucks with most of the contents of his store, he wondered what he should do with the rest. "Danny, after we load the trucks let's take down the sign as a precaution and lets load up these boxes, too," said Jim.

"Aren't those your federal forms?" asked Danny.

"They sure are and if it comes to it, they'll be fire starter."

Mary drove into the parking lot as the sign was being taken down. "Jim, you won't believe what I just saw in town!"

"Let me guess, cops everywhere and military vehicles?"

"How did you know?" Mary asked.

"Just a hunch..." said Jim. "We better get home, get the kids and get all we can before we head south." The three of them drove down the road to the house.

"You cannot enslave a free man; the most you can do is kill him."

- Robert Heinlein

Chapter Three: Run or Fight

When the three people turned their vehicles down Jim's street, they saw people at the house. Jim sped up. It was their friends and their families. Jim had told them all before that if there were ever an emergency, to get to his house. "Everyone listen up! We're going to get a few more things and be on our way. Matt, Rick and all that want to, arm up. Things might get crazy out there."

Like many people, Jim decided to stockpile ammo and food instead of gold and silver over the years. With ammo for your guns, you can take all the gold and silver you want. With food already stored, you won't lose your life trying to get some at the grocery store when others are rioting for it. Jim wasn't crazy, he was just practical. He'd spent eight years in Marines' infantry and reconnaissance units and was no stranger to preparedness. Jim hadn't been a Boy Scout, but you'd think he had been.

Growing up on a farm, the drill was get up early and do all your chores before school and hope you had time to eat breakfast before the bus came. Jim was glad for his childhood and knew that everything he had, he'd worked for. "You appreciate the things you have more when you work and sweat for them," he would tell his own kids all the time. "These kids you hang out with in and out of school, they don't know what work is and if their parents just keep giving them money and electronics, they won't know what to do in the real world," he told them.

Soon after spending his time serving his country, Jim headed for the "last frontier" to make his way in the world. Soon after, he met Mary, who had grown up in Alaska. It was love at first sight, even after the alcohol wore off. Between the two of them, they were ready.

After loading all the vehicles with guns, ammo and food, Jim got on his tactical vest and hooked his MSAR 5.56mm rifle to it, clipped the buckles of his Safariland drop leg holster for his 1911 .45 and was ready to go. The small bull pup rifle was perfect for driving down the road, attached to a vest with body armor. All of Jim's gear was customized for fit, function and maneuverability. "Everyone saddle up and lock and load."

A few of the woman and older kids had either handguns on their sides, rifles in their arms or both. The entire group was well trained with all of their weapons and gear. Everyone around town knew Mary and some of the other wives. It was nothing out of the ordinary to see one of them dragging their kids around the grocery store with a handgun on their hip.

Everyone got ready and into their vehicles for the evacuation. Mary took one last look at her house and yard before getting in the truck. "I hope this is all going to be okay," she said to Jim.

"Everything will be just fine, baby."

All of a sudden a Humvee was racing toward the house; everyone pointed their weapons at it. "Nobody shoot!" yelled Jim. "It's just Matt." He stopped and got out. "Boy, what the hell are you doing?" asked Jim. "Do you want to get shot?"

"I barely made it here, they're everywhere!"

Naythan was also turning in toward the house just as they started to talk to Matt.

"I know, and that's why we're leaving. Are you ready, do you have everything you need?" asked Jim.

"I was born ready!" said Matt.

Naythan got out of his truck, which was steaming from under the hood.

"Can I ride with you Matt?" asked Naythan.

Get in, said Matt.

"Ok everyone. Let's go. Matt, Naythan we're on channel two."

"Thanks, Jim," they said.

Matt was a young kid that loved guns. He would go into Jim's store all the time and order this or buy that. Matt reminded Jim of himself when he was that age. He wanted everything and spent all his money on stuff he thought he had to have right then. Naythan was a new friend to the group, but very well liked.

Jim led the convoy of seven vehicles down the road. People all over the subdivision and on the main road were frantic. They seemed confused. "I'm sure glad we have a plan," said Jim over the radio. All drivers were in contact by hand-held radios. Cell phones were not working and it was already in the plan to use the radios for that reason. Driving down the road, they could see big transport planes and parachutes in the sky.

"This doesn't look good..." said Matt. As they approached the first main intersection, they saw the flashing lights and military trucks.

"Everyone get ready, but stay calm," said Jim.

Jim rolled down his window and came to a stop. A man in camouflage clothing approached his truck. "What's going on, Hal?" asked Jim.

"We need to have you turn around and go home Jim. We don't want any trouble." Hal saw how Jim was dressed and knew the guns were loaded. The two men had a little history. Hal used to be a local cop and would give Jim grief over the smallest things. He would pull Jim over and make up things just to piss him off, because he ended up with Mary instead of Hal. Hal knew that Jim always had a gun or two with him at all times and would want to see them. Jim knew the law just as well, if not better, than any cop in the area. "There won't be any trouble as long as you move aside and let us through, bud. We are ready to fight, but would rather not." Hal knew Jim was serious. He relented, and it was the best decision.

"Let them through," said Hal. "Jim, the next check point won't be this easy."

"Kind of figured that," said Jim as he drove away.

"Everyone listen up," said Jim. "We may have to fight our way through the next road block." They continued down the road with everyone scanning the entire area for anything out of the ordinary.

At the end of a long straight stretch, Jim could see vehicles blocking the road. He picked up his binoculars to get a better view. "Yep," Jim said over the radio for everyone to hear. "We have blue hats in the distance with automatic vehicle mounted weapons. Rick, I want you to take your rifle into the tree line on the right flank and set up." The vehicles all stopped for Rick to slip out. Rick used to be on the Army's long distance shooting team years ago, and spent his four years as a sniper.

After he got out of the truck with his sniper rifle, a POF semi auto chambered in .308 caliber, the small convoy slowly made its way to the road block. Jim got out of his truck and went to talk to the soldiers. A few minutes later, a bottle of water that Jim had put on one of the Hummers blew up. Just then all of the soldiers pointed their weapons at Jim then slowly put them down, surrendering. Jim called for Matt and a few others to get out of the trucks. The soldiers started to walk past them back toward town. Jim and the other men collected all the weapons, took the machine guns off the vehicles, and punctured tires so the soldiers couldn't use the Hummers for a while. After everyone got loaded back up, they drove down the road a few hundred yards and picked up Rick. The group continued down the road toward the mountains.

The story everyone got from Jim afterward was that he told the commander of the U.N. forces on the road to surrender. After a small chuckle rang out from the soldiers, Jim placed his water bottle on the lead Hummer and radioed Rick to take it out. When the bottle blew up from the impact of the round hitting it, the soldiers pointed their weapons at Jim and the convoy. Jim calmly told them that the four snipers he had in the woods could easily take them all out before they could shoot back and they should surrender. Without knowing how many men were really out there, they gave up. This was typical for U.N. troops and they all hoped that the next time would be this easy.

After almost an hour of driving, the small convoy reached the southern peninsula town of Ninilchick where they met up with Bill and his son Terry. The small town was even more deserted than usual.

"What took you so long, Jim?" asked Bill.

"We ran into a few road blocks, but nothing we couldn't handle."

"Well..." said Bill "We better head up to the homestead before things get any worse."

"Lead the way," said Jim. The convoy followed Bill and Terry down the road. Bill had lived in the area for his entire life and Terry had grown up there, too. They were both Alaska Natives and had access to all of the hunting grounds that most Alaskans didn't. Most in the group had known Bill for years and Jim had sold him many guns; because of this everyone got to go hunting with him and Terry.

The way up into the Timber Wolf Mountains was a long, bumpy, gravel and dirt road with many curves. It took an hour and a half to reach the cabin that Bill owned at the base of the mountains. The cabin was off the beaten path and well secluded. It had a rustic Alaska look and was built with logs. It was a two story cabin with a full basement. This had been the base camp for their hunting trips for years. The vehicles were parked under the trees with camo netting thrown over them for concealment after all the food, ammo, guns and belongings were taken out of them.

The cabin was just the front of what was an elaborate maze of tunnels in an old gold mine. Bill owned the cabin and land, but everyone spent a lot of time in it. Bill let everyone come up not only for hunting season, but for family getaways or just a romantic getaway for two. It was a nice way to conceal the gold claim from thieves when it was still producing gold. The claim hadn't been active since Bill's grandfather ran it fifty years ago. They had all spent years going up there making rooms in the tunnels livable not only for hunting, but for emergencies like this.

The rooms had been carved out with jackhammers, picks and shovels. Miners that used to work the tunnels for gold had started the rooms so most of the digging was just finish work. The dirt and rock pulled out of the tunnels was taken outside and gone through. There was still gold in the mine, just not a whole lot. What gold the men found helped finance what they were doing. The tunnels and rooms were reinforced with concrete once they were fully dug out then finally finished with wood on the inside. The work was exhausting, but the reward of what they would have when finished made it worth it. They looked just like rooms in a regular house from inside. Quite a bit of time, energy and money went into putting everything together. They had electricity generated from a few windmills next to the cabin. They had buried bulk tanks for propane and gasoline. There were electric pumps attached to the tanks for easy pumping. They had enough food stored for ten plus years with minor consumption. The food was mainly Mountain House dehydrated cans and bags and had very long shelf lives as long as they were stored properly. Also, rice, beans, salt and other foods with the longest shelf lives were picked for extended storage. There were of course stacks of MREs that Jim got a good deal on and, being a Marine, he said they were a necessity. Water was abundant in the mountains any time of the year and just had to be filtered properly before consumption. The cabin had a well drilled beside it, but just in case there were plenty of filters if the electricity stopped for any reason. A few out buildings built into the mountain housed extra four wheelers and sleds as well as construction supplies. Bill was well known in the area and nobody ever messed with the stuff they had left up on the mountain. As each family settled in, the realization of what was going on was beginning to set in. Jim stopped by each room and said that everyone would join in on a get together in the morning to figure out the next step. The men in the group carried all of the ammo and weapons that had been brought with them and added them to the arsenal in the armory. The stockpile had been built up over the years with many weapons, but they each had their favorites.

The weapons in the armory varied anywhere from handguns to rifles and shotguns. Full combat gear with body armor lined one side. Thousands of rounds of ammo in boxes and ammo cans were stacked up in order of caliber.

"The machine guns that were taken from the U.N. troops on the way down look real good in the rack next to the other rifles!" said Matt as he helped put them away. Most of the guns and ammo had been purchased through Jim's store over the years. Everything was put away and they all went to their separate rooms to be with their families.

Chapter Four: Information

Everyone woke to far off explosions early the next morning, rocking their new living areas. Bill was running down the reinforced tunnels to make sure that everyone was alright. "What the hell is going on?" asked Jim as Bill got to his room.

"Terry is turning on the radio to see if we can get any news," said Bill.

As all the adults made their way into the cabin to find out what was happening, the explosions stopped. Terry was turning through the stations until he got to one he could understand.

"I'm...I'm told that Anchorage has been bombed by an unknown enemy," said the radio DJ. "We are still getting conflicting reports, but as far as we know Anchorage is gone."

"That's almost 400,000 people," said Rick. Everyone else was silent.

"Well," said Bill, "since nobody will get any more sleep maybe we should have that meeting and figure out what to do." Everyone agreed and sat around the big stone fireplace to come up with a plan.

Everyone started to bring up questions about what might be going on. Bill interrupted and said, "When we find out for sure we will know. Until then it's just speculation."

"We need to establish a perimeter," said Jim. Everyone agreed and plans were made to figure out what kind and how it would be made.

The next day, traps were made. They were set all around the cabin for a half mile in all directions over the course of the next week. Jim suggested that a map of the traps, and what kinds they were, should be drawn up for everyone so they could avoid them. They knew that animals could set off the traps as well as their new enemy, whoever that might be. The group practiced for different scenarios. If they were attacked, they would have to get their gear on and get into position according to where the enemy was coming from. Jim broke the men into teams so they were used to the same people. Designated snipers would move to positions accordingly. They still weren't sure about everything that was going on, but they were going to be prepared. They knew that U.N. troops were on U.S. soil, but why bomb Anchorage? Was it because of the Army and Air Force bases that were up there? Speculation was all that they had for now. They all knew that something might happen due to the shape of the world in recent years, but it would have to be bad in the U.S. to send in foreign troops, and that was an act of war. Where was the military and why was this being allowed to happen here? It was like a conspiracy, but it was real and happening.

Everyone agreed to send a few people into town two weeks after they had the area secured. They all got settled as well as possible and figured they were ready for most scenarios. They had been preparing this area for some time with wind and solar power. Now it was time to put all the preparations to the test. An observation post was built in a large group of trees. From the hidden post you could see for miles. There were a total of eighteen people living in the cabin and tunnels at this point, but only nine men to fight if it came down to it. The women and children could, but nobody wanted that.

Two hours before daylight on a cold, foggy day, four of the men went down the mountain on four wheelers using night vision goggles to see their way. The men wanted to be as stealthy as possible so no one would know where they came from. Just before they got to the first grocery store, they decided to stop and hide the four wheelers. After a few hours of hiding in the trees and watching with binoculars, they began to see people walk and drive around. Everything looked normal as far as they could tell, so they entered the store. The four men spread out into the store which was pretty empty of everything. Jim walked up to the counter to ask the clerk a few questions. "Excuse me, ma'am," asked Jim. "I don't mean to bother you, but I have been wandering around the mountains since my truck broke down and was wondering if you could tell me what is going on around here?"

The clerk had a funny look on her face and asked Jim if he was serious. He said, "Yes ma'am I am." She called him over to the side of the store to tell him all that she knew. After a few minutes, he shook her hand

and motioned for everyone to leave. They left the store much like they had come in, one at a time and in different directions.

After regrouping in the tree line down the road, Jim told the rest of the men what the clerk had said. Anchorage had not been bombed, but an electro magnetic pulse was set off to cripple the local populace. A few unlucky passenger jets had fallen out of the sky because of the electronics being fried.

The United Nations had sent in troops in order to keep the peace for the transition that was supposed to happen.

"What transition?" asked Rick.

"Well, I guess this is no longer the United States of America," said Jim.

"What the hell does that mean?" asked Terry.

"One World Government, One World Power ring any bells?"

"That's crazy!" said Rick.

"Well, it's happening and I'm glad we're prepared."

"I knew it would be an EMP," said young Matt. "I have been telling you guys that for years now. If they want our land and women, then bombing us would just be stupid. By setting off an EMP they could come in and take us over and we wouldn't be able to do much about it because all of our electronics would be useless."

"Well, it's a good thing they didn't set it off down here, buddy," said Jim.

Waiting for night to fall felt like an eternity. The men just sat under the trees and moved as little as possible. After it was pitch black, everyone put on their night vision goggles and got on their four wheelers to head back to the mountains to plan the next move. They had to run this way in order to make sure they weren't followed. As they made their way up the bumpy road, they saw flashes of light in the distance in all directions and they heard faint explosions and gunfire. They figured it was people opposing the U.N. troops. Jim turned on his radio. To let Bill know they were approaching he squelched it twice. IR light flashed back toward them twice to tell them that all was clear. They continued to the cabin and put the four wheelers away in the shed.

The men went inside the cabin to let the others know what they had learned. After getting washed up and getting something to eat, everyone sat around the big stone fireplace to let the rest know that they were in for a long winter.

"So," said Bill. "This is it? The world is being taken over now?"

"From the sounds of it, the countries are just being handed over to the United Nations coalition by the respective federal governments," said Jim.

"I'm not a conspiracy nut like you two, so can you spell it out for us?" asked Rick.

"This globalization has been going on for decades," said Bill. "It couldn't be done overnight, or there would be too much opposition. The newest thing is The National Defense Authorization Act for Fiscal Year 2012. It's a law in the United States that has hundreds of pages covering numerous topics. I will read you some of it; the most important parts really," said Bill.

Bill looked through his research as he addressed the group, picking out the important parts.

"The act primarily authorizes funding for the defense of the United States and its interests abroad; crucial services for service members and their families, and vital national security programs that must be renewed. The Act also contains critical administration initiatives to control the spiraling health care costs of the Department of Defense, to develop counterterrorism initiatives abroad, to build the security capacity of key partners, to modernize the force, and to boost the efficiency and effectiveness of military operations worldwide. The provisions which have received the most attention and generated the most controversy are contained in Title X, Subtitle D, and entitled 'Counter-Terrorism.' In particular, sub-sections 1031 and 1032 which deal with detention of persons the government suspects of involvement in terrorism and have generated controversy as to their legal meaning and their potential implications for abuse of Presidential authority. The detention provisions of the Act have received critical attention and raise concerns about the scope of the President's authority. This includes contentions that those who may be held indefinitely could include U.S. citizens arrested on American soil. U.N. Agenda 21 for the 21st Century is a major step, the International Small Arms Treaty and..."

"Wait," interrupted Susan, Rick's wife. "Isn't Agenda 21 just about the environment?"

"It goes way beyond that," said Jim. "The U.N. would like you to believe that's all it is, but in reality it covers everything on this planet. They want to control all aspects of your life, from the food you eat to the job you have and who you marry and so on."

"This is mega socialism on a global scale. We have all kinds of other literature around here somewhere," said Bill. He rifled through some of his cabinets and pulled out an article.

In 1987, Vice President of the World Socialist Party Gro Harlem Brundtland wrote a report for the United Nations entitled "Our Common Future" which explained that environmentalism could be used as a tool to control all the people of the world and establish a one-world government.

According to the authors of Agenda 21, the objective of sustainable development is to integrate economic, social and environmental policies in order to achieve reduced consumption, social equity and the preservation and restoration of biodiversity. Sustainablists insist that every societal decision be based on environmental impact, focusing on three components, global land use, global education, and global population control and reduction.

"This started with 'eminent domain,'" said Bill.

"What is that?" asked Mary.

"I will read you the definition," said Bill. "'The property of subjects is under the eminent domain of the state, so that the state or he who acts for it may use and even alienate and destroy such property, not only in the case of extreme necessity, in which even private persons have a right over the property of others, but for ends of public utility, to which ends those who founded civil society must be supposed to have intended that private ends should give way. But, it is to be added that when this is done the state is bound to make good the loss to those who lose their property.' Essentially it means if they want what you have, they will take it."

"Here is some more information that you also all need to hear," said Bill.

"Following the establishment of the Council on Sustainable Development, J. Gary Lawrence, Council advisor to President Clinton, revealed: Participating in a UN advocated planning process would very likely bring out many of the conspiracy-fixated groups and individuals in our society. This segment of our society which fears one-world government and a U.N. invasion of the United States, through which our individual freedom would be stripped away, would actively work to defeat any elected official who joined the conspiracy by undertaking LA21 [Local Agenda 21]. So we call our process something else, such as comprehensive planning, growth management or smart growth."

"This can't be happening," said Susan.

"Well, it is," said Jim. "This has been a hidden plan for the world and that is what all of this is for." Jim pointed to the cave entrance behind them. "The move to a one world government, one world power has been carefully planned, slowly conditioning people, moving them step-by-step toward public acceptance of it."

"I knew some of you were skeptical, so we made this a weekend getaway and hunting camp, too. This all has become a reality whether we like it or not," said Bill.

Just about everyone went to bed, stunned and in disbelief. "I know you have talked about this stuff before," Mary said to Jim. "But, I truly didn't believe it all until now."

"Well," said Jim. "I didn't want to believe it but would rather be prepared just in case."

"A democracy cannot exist as a permanent form of government. It can only exist until the voters discover that they can vote themselves largesse from the public treasury. From that moment on, the majority always votes for the candidates promising the most benefits from the public treasury with the result that a democracy always collapses over loose fiscal policy, always followed by a dictatorship."

—Alexander Fraser Tyler (1770)

Chapter Five: Reality

The next morning as everyone got up, the men with radios heard them squelch three times. This meant that they had company.

Rick and Jim went up front to the cabin to ask Bill, who was keeping guard, what was going on.

"It's the local law," said Bill. The Alaska State Troopers slowly made their way up to the cabin in a cruiser. Two men in military fatigues got out. Bill walked out to greet them. After a few short minutes, Bill said, "You two need to leave." They would not go away and wanted to go inside the cabin.

Just as they approached the front, Terry went out and said, "Dad, we going to eat or what?" The troopers stopped as they could see that Bill was not alone.

"We will be back," said the tall trooper.

"You are not welcome on my property," said Bill.

"We will see about that," said the shorter and more muscular trooper. They turned around and drove away.

At breakfast Bill said out loud but not really talking to anyone, "I guess it's the beginning of the end."

"What do you mean, dad?" asked Terry.

"He means they are turning on their own people, son," said Jim. "This is what we all have been preparing for, for so many years. We had hoped it would never happen, but we built all this just in case it did. Now, we will just sit back and watch and hope it doesn't impact our lives too much."

"What if the troopers come back or bring more men?" asked Terry.

"We will handle each situation as it is presented to us," said Jim.

As a group, everyone decided to put out remote cameras along with the traps that had been put in place around the perimeter. They also decided to put some at the main intersections of the road heading up to the cabin. They positioned the cameras around the cabin, but figured they would be of better use further out for advanced warning.

The resident computer nerd, Jessie, attached infrared lasers to the cameras with motion alarms that would start recording so everyone would see what was coming their way. They had someone monitoring the camera feeds 24/7 in order to be ready for anything.

As soon as the cameras were activated by motion, they would start recording on an external hard drive and be erased weekly if nothing had happened.

Two days later in the early morning hours, about four a.m., everyone got knocks on their doors.

"We have had motion at the road junction about two miles away."

"Show me," said Jim as he walked into the cabin. Rick kept a live feed going and at the same time pulled up the video from the time the alarm had gone off. "I see two Alaska State Trooper SUVs and a five ton truck with who knows what or how many men."

"Everyone get your gear on, this is not a drill!" Jim took control as usual because it came so naturally to him, being a former Marine. Most valued his leadership; some questioned it, but at the end of the day were all glad he was there.

"I want two snipers in elevated positions. Matt here and Rick here," Jim pointed at the hand drawn map of the cabin and perimeter. "Team one take the left flank, team two, the right. Just as we have practiced people! Now move!" Everyone grabbed their rifles and gear. Most of the rifles were AK-47s because of the reliability and large caliber compared to the AR-15. A child could shoot the rifle, so it was especially deadly in trained hands.

Everyone had barely gotten into position when the vehicles approached. Bill met them from the cabin deck and shined a three million candlelight power spotlight at them. "That's far enough!" yelled Bill. The tall trooper from before moved closer and a warning shot was fired at his feet.

Not even flinching, the trooper said in a loud voice, "By the power given to me by the United Nations..." Just then, twenty or so armed men jumped out of the five ton truck and lined up by the trooper. "You will surrender and have your cabin searched," he continued.

Bill said, "This is your last chance. You surrender or you will not see the sun rise today." Laughter broke out among the men the trooper brought. Bill shut off the bright spotlight and gunfire erupted down from the flanks. Naythan fired his homemade cannon at the vehicles and they were shredded by the shrapnel that he had loaded it with. As the windows of the vehicles shattered, glass flew everywhere. Jim and the rest of the men were sending a message. The U.N. troops and the trooper didn't even have time to fire a round before they were gunned down. The firefight only lasted a few minutes, but for most it seemed like an eternity. No one had killed a man before and it felt like a dream. The justification was that they were defending their families and country.

"Rick," said Jim. "I want you to sweep the area with the thermal monocular, please."

"Got one," said Rick. "Two hundred yards to the southwest, I see a lone man."

"Take him out!" ordered Jim. "Team one move to intercept, use NVGs."

A lone shot cut through the silent night. "He's down," said Rick. "Team one; he is right in front of you just behind that tree."

"We see him, he is still alive. Looks like you shot right through the tree."

"Bring him up to the cabin and let's clean this mess up," said Jim.

The men had about an hour to strip off gear and firearms and load all the bodies in the vehicles. They got done just as the first glimmer of light could be seen above the mountains. The plan was to drive the vehicles down the mountain to an old cabin and make it look like the firefight had been there instead.

Half of the men took the vehicles and bodies down to the old cabin and torched it with the dead men in it. The smoke would be seen for miles and the people that found them later would hopefully think it had all happened there.

"When injustice becomes law, then resistance becomes duty."

-Thomas Jefferson

Chapter Six:
Interrogation

The man that had been behind the tree that Rick shot through was the second trooper. He had a SAT phone in his hand and was trying to dial when team one found him. He had a 7.62 round and wood splinters in his chest. He was lucky that the tree had absorbed most of the bullet's energy, but not lucky he had been found. "We have a few questions for you, pal," said Jim. He didn't say a thing until Jim pressed on his chest wound.

"AAHHH!" the trooper yelled. "I can't tell you anything!" he said. "If I do, they will do much more to me than you could. I have seen what they have done to people that won't submit."

"Well, then you clearly have underestimated us, slick," said Little Matt. "I was trained to interrogate by the best mercenaries in the world. You're in for a world of hurt if you don't start talking."

The trooper was blindfolded and taken down into the cave system to an uncompleted room. "Get me a chair and some flexi cuffs," Jim told Terry. They placed the trooper in the center of the room and secured him to the chair. "Alright now Smith," Jim called him by the name on his uniform. "I want to know why this area has been targeted by the military."

"I told you, I will say nothing, so you might as well kill me now."

"Not going to happen...yet," said Jim. Smith felt a sharp pain just above his right heel as Matt severed the achilles tendon. Smith was screaming. Jim used a propane torch to cauterize the wound and the screaming continued. "I'm going to let you think about everything for a few minutes," said Jim. "When I get back, you are either going to talk or feel more pain. You have my word that if you cooperate, I won't kill you."

Jim, Matt and Rick left the room. Danny walked up to them from down the hall and asked if they needed any help. "We have it all under control, Danny," said Jim. "You want to get Bill and cut some meat off that last moose you guys shot? We can throw some steaks on the grill tonight."

"I can do that," said Danny, and he walked back to the cabin.

"What the hell are you doing, just going medieval on him?" asked Rick. "I'm with you, but this is wrong. We need to talk to him and find out what we can. He is already wounded, why make it worse?"

"Do you think I want to be out here with my family?" asked Jim. "Hell no, I want to be back home in my recliner drinking a beer and watching TV. But guess what? We are here and need to deal with the fact that they are trying to kill us."

"You know we can't let him live," said Jim. "I said I wouldn't kill him guys, but I said nothing about anyone else. We need to get as much info out of him as we can and then you two can take him for a ride."

"Sounds good to me," said Matt.

Ten minutes had past and the three men went back to the room. Smith had passed out so Matt splashed some water in his face to wake him up. He woke up screaming, then saw it wasn't a dream. "Are you ready to answer our questions?" asked Jim.

"How can I trust that you won't kill me like you say?" asked Smith.

"You can't," said Jim. "You need to tell us why you came to the cabin. Were you looking for someone?"

"Yes..." said Smith.

"Well don't make me guess, boy!"

"Okay! We were looking for you. Your names are Jim Stanton, Matthew Woods and Richard Perry."

The three men looked at each other and almost at the same time they said, "How the hell did you know that?"

"Your names, as well as many others, are on a high priority terrorist watch list."

"Are you calling us terrorists?" asked Matt. "We're American's just like you, you son of a bitch!"

"Calm down big boy..." said Jim.

"Can I talk to you for a minute?" asked Matt. Jim followed him out into the hall and closed the door.

"Look," said Matt, "I know you guys just want him to talk but I think extreme measures need to be taken."

"I think we've given him something to think about already buddy, let's just see what happens, okay?" said Jim.

They both walked back into the room. Matt was ready for anything and wanted to get to the bottom of things.

"Start from the beginning, Smith. We want to hear it all," said Jim.

"Can I have some water?" he asked.

"Matt, give him some water please."

"This better be good..." said Matt. He reluctantly gave Smith some water from his bottle.

"Ok..." started Smith. "A few weeks ago we, as in all the troopers on the Peninsula, were called in for an emergency meeting. We were surprised to see men in military fatigues at the front of the room. A man with a French accent told us to be seated. He said he was with the United Nations and that we were all now under his command. Many of us were not happy and started asking questions, but the captain of the post told us to be quiet. The military man told us of a new age coming to our country and that we should all be glad to be a part of it. I heard troopers shout things like, 'you can go to hell' and 'not me!' Half of the men in the room got up and left. For the men that stayed in their seats, the military man said that this was to be expected. 'Those of you that now occupy this room, you are the right men for the job,' he said. I can't forget any of this," said Smith, "because I still can't believe it."

"So," Matt said. "Why go along with all this if you don't think that way?"

"The U.N. generals had the troopers that left that day killed as an example for the rest of us. Even their families were killed. I don't want to do this to my fellow Americans, but you have to draw a line and decide what is right for your family."

Smith had some good points, thought Jim, *but the founding fathers of this great nation had some, too.*

"Well, I really think that you decided poorly. I would give up my life for my family, and to defend this country from all enemies, foreign and domestic. I will not sit idly by while our freedoms are stripped from us, or let this great nation be wiped from the earth!" Jim was not happy.

"Mr. Smith, you have committed treason against this country," said Jim. "You cannot be allowed to spread your poison to the masses."

"Wait!" said Smith. "I...I...thought you said you wouldn't kill me?"

"I will keep my word, but these men never said they wouldn't."

"No, no, you can't do this! My wife, my children," said Smith.

"They will not be harmed by us," said Jim. "We are not the enemy, we are patriots. Get this trash out of here guys." Rick and Matt took Smith for a drive. He no longer fought back; he must have finally realized the mistake he had made. Smith left without another word.

Matt and Rick came back two hours later. Jim asked, "How did it go?"

"He said he was sorry," said Matt as he walked into the cabin.

"Those who trade liberty for security have neither."

—John Adams

Chapter Seven: Us or Them

The men continued to watch, listen and wait. Some of the group was growing impatient. They knew what was happening yet they did nothing to stop it. What could they do? They could take the fight to the enemy or they could continue doing nothing and hope things got better on their own. *I'm sure that's what most of the men think,* thought Jim. Mary had always been the one that would listen and give advice, but she had been very quiet lately. She knew that Jim wouldn't let anything happen to her, the kids, or anyone in the group if he could help it, but she was still uneasy about the whole situation.

Every once in a while they caught someone attempting to sneak through the perimeter, desperately explaining how bad it was in town. People were being beaten or shot on the streets. They had no choice but to send them away and hope they didn't tell the U.N. where they were. These were locals, but how long could they hold out, especially with winter coming? This place was ready, but were the people in town or elsewhere? They hoped to add on to the tunnel system soon and make more rooms. They needed more people to make this happen, but who could they trust and how would they feed them? A plan was being put together to figure out how to do what they needed in the mountain and how to supply everyone. Bill was the one heading up the project with the help of Jessie and her computer skills. Jessie was big Matt's daughter. Matt had been a corrections officer before all of this happened. Jessie was just out of high school and was hoping to attend a technical college to become a computer technician.

They had already been attacked once. Was it planned because they knew everyone was in this cabin or were random checks being made of citizens?

The perimeter security was the best they could manage with the man power and the resources that they had. They needed to make it better, and they would do the best they could to defend their friends and families.

Bill was working on the main plans for the cave system and Rick was in charge of security and the future plans for the perimeter. This was to be their home until things got better and they could go back to their real homes. No one knew when, or if, that would ever happen. Everyone made the best of things the way they were.

"Perimeter alert," came across the radio.

"What is it Bill, another local?" asked Matt.

"Not this time boys. This looks like the real deal, armored vehicles and troop transports."

"Rick, grab the .50 cal this time," said Jim. "I want you 500 yards southeast of the cabin to draw their fire away from team two. Team one; I want you 100 yards southeast of the pits. We will draw them in and pick them off."

"Matt, I want you and Little Matt to set up here and here. I want you displacing after every two rounds," said Jim. "What do you think, Bill?"

"I think one of our wandering friends got paid, that's what I think."

"I need you and Terry this time," said Jim. "Go into the tree position and don't start firing until they advance on team one. Rick, this will confuse them and hopefully we will get them all very quickly. Don't compromise your position, take out a few and stop until they advance again."

They were ready, or so they thought. The vehicles stopped short of the cabin and all the troops got out. Jim lost count at 50 or so. Most of the men had never killed a human being before this all started. Avid hunters they were, but not human killers. A few in the group had been in conflicts like Iraq or Afghanistan, but not much combat experience.

The troops were fanning out and advancing. That's when they started to engage. The turret gunners on the vehicles were the first to go and then the officers. This was working out great for Bill and Terry from their elevated position in the trees. None of the U.N. troops even knew they were there. They were dropping like flies.

This was survival, and that's how they had to view it. Just when they thought they had it easy, an attack helicopter came out of nowhere. Door gunners sprayed team one. They couldn't afford to lose anyone. As team one and Rick were put out of action by the helicopter, the U.N. troops advanced even faster on their position. As fast as it appeared, the helicopter was shot down. Because of the chaos, no one could tell at first who or what shot it down. As Jim made his way by the cabin on the heels of the troops, he could see what had done it. Jim's oldest boy, Kyle, had joined the fight and turned the tides. He had assembled Jim's Barrett .50 BMG and shoulder fired it at the helicopter. Three rounds struck it in the engine and rotor shaft and it started smoking and spinning out of control. The helicopter managed to fly a few hundred more yards before hitting the ground hard and exploding.

The U.N. troops were being engaged from three different directions and were confused. Little Matt had stopped sniping and was walking straight at the remaining troops and firing like crazy. He just kept pushing forward, only stopping to drop to a knee to reload or to throw hand grenades he had picked up from the last engagement. Jim couldn't believe his eyes. They continued to engage the enemy until there was no more resistance. Empty shell cases, blood and bodies were all over the place. They went through the kill zone to finish off the wounded. As they made their way to Rick and team one, Jim could see that not all of the men had been so lucky.

Eric, Rick's oldest son, had been shot. "Rick, you need to get down here!" said Jim.

"On my way," said Rick. The boy wasn't in immediate danger, the bullet had missed his lungs but the exit wound tore up his shoulder. He would need antibiotics, but they had none.

"Team two, start the cleanup and we'll get Eric inside," said Jim. They used quick clot on both sides of the wound to stop the bleeding, but they would need a doctor. He had to be brought to the mountain; they couldn't risk taking Eric to town and possibly getting captured. They couldn't hide this battle very well, but did the best they could to make it look like it happened on the other side of the mountain. The bodies of the enemy troops were loaded onto the trucks after they were searched and all weapons, ammo, and grenades were taken off of them. The men drove the vehicles that would still run and towed the rest.

Chapter Eight: New Friends

Bill, Terry and Jim left late that night for town the usual way with NVGs on four wheelers. Jessie saw them pass the last remote perimeter camera. Then all was silent. Everyone stayed off radios unless it was necessary. With the technology that the U.N. had, they could pinpoint the position and just send in a missile.

Bill knew the local doctor, but would he help? Would he still be alive?

They made it to the clinic well before dawn. If they could find him right away, they could get back up the mountain before daylight gave them up. The Doc was Alaska Native and most people had a hard time pronouncing his name, so Doc worked. His house was next to the clinic. Bill went to his door because he knew him. The doctor's wife, Lisa, answered the door after a few knocks.

"Who is it?" she asked.

"It's Bill Miller, ma'am. We need the doc."

"Just a minute," she said.

The doctor came to the door still half asleep. "What is so damn important?" he asked.

"Sir, we have a friend that needs medical attention, but we couldn't bring him to you."

"Why the hell not?" he asked. "Do you know what time it is, son?"

"Yes sir, I do and I wouldn't bother you at this hour if it wasn't important."

"Well, since I'm up what's wrong?"

"It's a gunshot and it's bad," said Bill." Doc knew Bill wouldn't have come if it wasn't important.

"Lisa, can you please get my bag and make sure it has meds in it. Don't tell anyone where I am. Tell them I am fishing," said the doctor. The four of them got on the four wheelers and disappeared into the darkness.

The ride back to the compound went a little slower with a rider. Finally, just before dawn, they made it to within visual distance. They sent a few squelches from the radio, then saw the flashes of IR light as planned. The men rode the four wheelers up to the cabin and Doc got off. After putting the vehicles away they went in to see how Eric was doing.

"What do you think, Doc?" asked Jim as they all walked into the room.

"Well, this isn't pretty, but I think I can fix him up." After working on Eric for a few hours, and getting a pint of blood each from some of the group that were compatible with his blood type, the doctor needed some rest.

"We'll take you back tonight," said Bill.

After some much needed sleep, they had a meeting with everyone in the group to discuss things like security, recruiting and resisting the U.N. The only way they could defend the stronghold against anything bigger than what they had recently done was to have more people themselves.

"This is our country," said Rick. "We need to organize a militia and go kick their asses."

"I agree," said Jim, "This conflict has already come knocking and we can't continue to sit by and hope it doesn't come back."

"There is a back way into the cave system further to the west. With a lot of effort and more people, we can occupy and fortify that end. We can keep the cabin separate from the rest and access it underground. We need to see if Doc wants to do the recruiting from town," said Bill. "We will have to train and organize people. Food, water and supplies will be a priority. We have guns and ammo from what we've recovered so far and can continue to scavenge," said Jim.

"I say we find a convoy to hit," said Matt. "That will send a message and then we can get people to join us."

They got information about a supply convoy heading south two days from then from Anchorage. They didn't know how reliable it was, but had to try and take it. They were told that it would be lightly guarded. They didn't know what the convoy would be carrying, so they had to make good shots on the soldiers and not the cargo. The convoy consisted of four trucks. There were two five-tons in the middle and a Humvee in the front and rear. The plan was to set the ambush on a deserted stretch of road so reinforcements would take a while to get there.

It was a calm and crisp mid-October morning. The men had staged a car wreck just past a corner in the highway. They hoped the soldiers would stop and not just try to run through it. They had people in the wrecked cars and on both sides of the road.

The convoy stopped and the turret gunners of the Humvees started scanning. Simultaneously, they took out the turret gunners and the drivers of all of the vehicles. They continued to engage the soldiers as they approached. They heard screams coming from one of the five-ton trucks. Very carefully, they pulled back the back cover. It was full of civilians. "Well at least we know what they were transporting..." said Rick.

"This one has guns, ammo and food!" said Matt.

"We don't have much time", said Jim. "Why are you people in this truck?"

"We were all woken up in the middle of the night. They put hoods on our heads and put us in this truck. We weren't told where we were going. I heard one of them mention a labor camp," said a lady.

"Okay," said Jim, "all of you out of the truck and help with the supplies."

"What are we doing?" asked Rick looking at the people.

"We will figure out what to do with them soon, but for now we have to leave," replied Jim. They torched the trucks and carried all the supplies they could back toward the mountains.

After an hour of walking, the new people started to drop stuff and said they couldn't go on. "Okay, time to take a break," said Matt, who was on point. "How is everyone doing?"

Matt questioned the civilians. Most of them complained that their feet hurt and that they were cold.

"Well," said Jim. "They really aren't dressed for this. These two women have slippers on. I want everyone to get under cover and huddle together for now." The dozen people did what they were asked.

"Base this is Mongoose, over," said Jim

"Go ahead Mongoose, over," said Bill.

"I need a few four wheelers and trailers to head our way, over."

"Roger that. Uh, where are you? Over," replied Bill.

"We are two clicks south of checkpoint two, Mongoose out."

Jim and Bill had come up with radio codes. They didn't want to be on the radio at all, but if the enemy was listening then they wouldn't know what they were talking about.

"I want blankets and whatever else you might have for these people to stay warm. I want a 360 perimeter set up around them with two per spot in 25 yard dispersion. Give me 50 percent alert until the rides come."

A few hours later the four wheelers showed up with Danny in the lead. "That boy wants to be a part of something so bad he's going to get himself, or someone else, killed," Rick said to Jim.

"We need all the people we can get and we will put them in the positions we see best," said Jim. "Some of you have had concerns about little Matt, but the truth is that kid has a lot of potential and I am going to stand by him and his Blackwater training. He walks into every situation like he knows what is coming next and I find that invaluable."

They loaded as many people as they could and all the supplies. They went on ahead and a small patrol followed until they could come back for them, too.

Chapter Nine: Dilemma

After a few trips, all of them were back at the cabin. Bill was instructed to not let anyone see the bunker cave system. He made room for the new people. After they got settled, they started asking questions like, "Are you taking me back to my family?" and "Can you check on my daughter? she was still at home when they took me." Families had been broken up and parents were taken away from their kids.

"We are not the military; we are a group of Alaskans fighting for our freedom. Now, I need to know why you were taken," said Jim. "One by one, I need to know full names, history, family size and occupation." As they went around the room, many military veterans spoke up. There was a machinist, a doctor, and other professionals. Bill was also a machinist and started talking to the new man.

The new people were told that they could stay in the out buildings until the cave could be set up to house them if they wanted to stay. Some people didn't like the idea of living underground until they were reminded about possible airstrikes. "We will be safe," said Bill. "We will reinforce the walls and ceiling."

"We need to know why they were rounded up," said Matt.

"We'll get to that," said Jim. One guy wouldn't stop asking questions like where they were and how many they had in their group.

"What's your name, buddy?" asked Matt.

"It's Mike, why?"

"You're asking a lot of questions, Mike. Why are you so interested?"

"Just am. What's wrong with getting to know the people that rescued us?"

"That's not what you're doing, Mike! You're asking specific questions related to our little home. Who are you really?" Matt shouted. Mike started to get up and Jim was on him.

"Easy fella, now why don't you come with me?" They put a hood over his head and took him into the makeshift interrogation room. After taking his hood off, Jim said, "Now strip."

"What?" asked Mike.

"I said strip boy, or we will do it for you!" Jim demanded. He started taking his clothes off and a knife fell out of his pants.

"Well look here!" said Rick. "How the hell did you get this on that truck if you were abducted? What is this tattoo?"

"Looks German," said Jim. "Hog tie him to the chair boys. We need to perform another interrogation."

Matt went to see if he could do some research and figure out what the tattoo was. As he was looking through a laptop on a secure server, Bill walked by.

"Why are you looking up a German Special Forces tattoo, Matt?" asked Bill.

"How do you know what it is?"

"I was stationed in Germany while I was in the Army a hundred years ago."

"Well, it turns out that our new friend has one of these."

"So, we have a mole..." said Bill.

"It appears so," Matt replied bleakly.

As soon as Jim got the information on the tattoo, he went to town on Mike. "Do you know what you're doing, man?" asked Rick.

"I saw this on a movie; I think its called water boarding." Jim winked at Rick. "Can you help me, Matt? Matt here is an expert at water boarding, buddy. He says that no one has ever drowned."

"No, no!" said Mike. "I am only here because I was ordered to find the missing assault group that was sent into the mountains to find insurgents."

"Do we look like insurgents?" asked Matt. "We are Americans and you are on our land. You are the insurgents, you bastard."

"So, how did you happen to be in the truck with all the others?" questioned Rick.

"One of us is always in the trucks loaded with people who have been ordered to re-education."

"What the hell is that?" asked Rick. "Let me guess, the people you want control of have something you want right?"

"I have a bigger question," said Jim. "Why are you volunteering information? We had an American law enforcement official in here recently and he didn't want to cooperate. Why are you helping us?"

"I don't think we belong here," said Mike.

"So you are just going to help us, why? Will it help you sleep better at night, or are you playing us?"

"I really want to help. I can give you radio frequencies, patrol routes, supply routes and troop strength."

"Give us something to verify and we will continue to keep you alive. Unless we decide we are being set up," demanded Jim.

Whoever the guy was, he came through with radio frequencies and patrol routes. All were verified, but Jim was still uneasy. After a while, things didn't pan out the way Mike said they would. His response was that the U.N. would change frequencies, patrol routes and times to avoid ambushes.

Jessie, the computer tech, said she could design a small bug that they could surgically insert into Mike to track him. "If we let him go to get more info, they would wonder where he had been. They could sweep him for bugs, too."

"Is there any way to turn it on and off?" asked Jim.

"No, the best we could do is to try and delay its activation long enough so when they sweep him, it's not on yet," replied Jessie.

"Okay Mike, if you really do want to help us then we need you to become a spy."

"I can do that, but how will I contact you? Do you want me to come back here?"

"Hell no, we will have to communicate through code on the radio. We will give you a code sheet to work with and frequencies. You will have to hide it internally, because they will pat you down."

"I'll do whatever you need me to do," said Mike.

"Okay, you leave tomorrow, and tonight we drink." Bill got out a few glasses and poured some whiskey for everyone. A few minutes after Mike took a drink he fell out of his chair. "Alright Jessie, get to work..."

The bug was inserted just below the skin between his shoulder blades. They took him down the mountain and propped him up against the side of the local market. He would be awake before he froze. They waited and watched from two hundred yards away. As soon as he woke up, Mike made his way toward the north end of town to the nearest U.N. check point. Jim and the guys saw them take Mike into the building by the road and that was it, for now.

"Conviction is worthless unless it is converted into conduct."

—Thomas Carlyle

Chapter Ten : Construction

With more people pouring in to help fight we need to build more rooms and buildings, Jim thought. The mountains were well known for the cabins locals enjoyed in summer and winter, so to see more people coming up hopefully just looked like common citizens were getting away from the violence. They were as careful as possible with the new people and security. They screened the newcomers the best they could, but with most not having any identification it was hard. Who was a spy and who was legitimate?

They built multiple perimeters falling back up the mountain to the cave entrance. There were bunkers built throughout the perimeter to allow for supply stockpiles and shelter for those on watch. On paper, the mountain looked like it was stepped, like rice fields in Asia. From the ground or air, it just looked like a few cabins. They used all natural materials to conceal the bunkers as well as the fighting positions. The cabins were really just decoys. They used them a little, but the main camp was inside the mountain stronghold, for so many reasons. The caves were much safer against possible bombardment;

they were insulated for all weather conditions and could house dozens of people. More room could be made if needed later. The original occupants were gold miners. They didn't live in the caves, but provided a good starting point to build from.

The main room was huge and provided a nice staging area. Multiple tunnels went on through the mountain and rooms were built off of them. They used steel and wood to reinforce the ceiling and walls of the rooms and tunnels.

They luckily had very few issues with water seepage. With the wind and solar energy they had running into the cave, they were able to keep the dampness very low. They were able to run dehumidifiers with the electricity in most rooms. They reused the water collected in the dehumidifiers along with the water in the filter system for washing and drinking. By doing this, less water had to be brought in from the outside. A staging area for combat operations was set up, a kitchen and dining area and a restroom and shower area, too. The gray water was piped outside to a septic tank and leach field that was built by plumbers in the group.

They made recon trips into town on a regular basis for information and brought back people and supplies. The men brought in people that could help in some way or that had nowhere to go. They couldn't just offer sanctuary to everyone or they would risk putting the compound in danger. They felt good about how they helped and how they planned to help, by taking back the country from the invaders. The people with skills or degrees in certain areas were put into groups after the screening process. They had carpenters, engineers, welders, plumbers and of course Jim's favorite, machinists. Bill was the best machinist they had. He could build anything. Bill had made the silencers for all of the weapons. The sniper rifles, machine guns and handguns all had them if they needed them. They made the men and weapons multi-mission capable. Indoors or outdoors, the snipers couldn't be seen at all. This allowed them to continue to engage without displacing as much.

They continued to get valuable information from the spy in the U.N. ranks. They would send out patrols to ambush convoys and get supplies. It was getting harder as winter pressed on and the snow got deeper, even with snow shoes and sleds. As February approached, they were running low on supplies with more than fifty people to care for.

A few of the men that had recently come to the community put together a trap line to take advantage of small animals for food and pelts for clothing. They were good at it too, bringing back wolves, foxes, lynx, martin and squirrels. Not everything they brought back was edible, but all the pelts made nice clothing and blankets.

The plan to plant crops in the spring seemed so far away. Every once in a while a foot patrol came across a moose and brought it back. It was easier with the snow shoes everyone had now than it had been in the beginning. The U.N. troops had nice snow shoes and the militia was glad to get them. Even though there was a lot of meat at first, it didn't last long with so many mouths to feed. With the cold winter, most everyone stayed inside the cave unless they were part of the militia and had to go on a patrol or stand sentry duty on the perimeter. Some of the adults set up a classroom for the kids. This was to allow them to continue on learning and have a sense of normalcy, and to keep them out of trouble.

Lucky for everyone, the weather broke in mid-March and they had an early spring upon them. They would be able to plant crops sooner and go further to get supplies and to take out more enemy troops.

"The tree of liberty must be refreshed from time to time with the blood of patriots and tyrants."

-Thomas Jefferson

Chapter Eleven: Enemy Lines

At some point they needed to push back and establish some lines. The main problem with defending anything was that the enemy had armor, artillery and air support. What did this group have but just a few dozen tired, broken, and hungry patriots? Jim's mind was swimming with all of this. *We have come so far in such a short time, but will it be enough?* Jim pondered.

One of the main problems was the lack of information. They had no idea what was happening outside of their immediate area. Was there really no U.S. military anymore? Did they all give in to the pressure of the U.N., or did some commanders stand and fight? The bottom line was they needed help.

They got word from their contact that a big convoy full of supplies and very few troops was on its way down from Anchorage. They would need most of the trained combat personnel that they had to pull off an interception. No one liked the idea of leaving the compound unprotected. After getting the whole group together, except the men Jim already talked to on perimeter security, the plan was outlined and the women and older children were given security tasks. Some were reluctant, but as it was explained to them, that if this wasn't done then they would starve, they finally came to their senses.

The combat patrol set off in the early morning hours toward their objective. The plan was to take control of the convoy and set up a line of defense within the closest town.

Upon arrival, they set up a kill zone and put snipers in place to provide over watch.

The trucks were more or less on time. As soon as the lead vehicle entered the kill zone, a claymore mine detonated. The convoy stopped and as the turret gunners in the Humvees opened up on both sides, the snipers went to work. The main force would stay back and under cover until given the order to advance. Naythan started shooting the containers of Tanerite binary explosives he had put beside the road. The additional explosions confused the U.N. troops even more.

The U.N. troops didn't know what was happening. The turret gunners were down and the drivers of the vehicles had been taken as well. Just as the ground forces were given the order to advance and secure the vehicles, two attack helicopters rose from below the bluff. Jim's men hadn't known they were there, waiting until the full force of the men attacked. Jim and the rest of the snipers engaged the helicopters. They made strafing runs and were harder to hit. Everyone just kept firing.

Finally, one was hit and slammed into the ground. The other helicopter paused to attack the sniper that downed the other. Everyone opened up with more sniper and automatic fire. The helicopter limped over the bluff and crashed into the beach.

"This is sierra one to all call signs. Recover what you can and fall back. Leave no man behind!" said Jim. They killed the rest of the U.N. soldiers in the convoy with a vengeance.

Young Matt got up on one of the Humvees, raised his rifle and yelled as loud as he could, "Wolverines!" and got back down.

The vehicles were searched and found that they were empty. The men quickly gathered weapons, ammo and the wounded men.

"What the hell was that back there?" Jim asked Matt.

"It had to be done," said Matt. "It was the appropriate thing to say at that point."

"I have to slightly agree with you," said Jim. "I loved that movie too, but now we need to go."

There were three men wounded and two dead as a result of the ambush. They hastily put together a combat patrol and moved out. They were a half click off the road when they heard and felt loud explosions. They dropped to the ground and saw the trucks blow up as two jets raced by, followed by two more. The lead jets were attacking the trucks and, more than likely, the militia if they had still been there. They got into some thick alders to hide and watch. They were witnessing a dog fight between what they hoped were attacking U.S. Air Force jets and the U.N. The fight didn't last long and the remaining jets flew off. The men continued on when the threat was gone.

Rick was on point and front security. He broke radio silence to say that he saw parachutes. The jets were gone and they had wounded to get back to safety. As they made their way up the mountain, they were very cautious. They walked for about forty-five minutes when Rick's hand went up to halt the patrol. Rick was still on point with Jim close behind when a yell rang out. "FROSTHEAVE, FROSTHEAVE!" said the voice.

Everyone was motionless. It was a challenge word and they didn't have the other one.

Jim said, "We are American citizens and we mean you no harm." They were suddenly surrounded by camouflaged troops pointing their weapons at them.

One of them moved to the front. "I am Captain Dan McGee First Force Recon U.S.M.C. And you are?"

"Are you part of the U.N. forces?" asked Jim.

"I'm asking the questions here!" said McGee.

"We are starving American citizens and doing what we can to survive. We have had a long winter. We have dead and wounded to take care of. Now, either help us or engage us! Your choice, Devil Dog," said Jim.

Stunned, the captain asked, "You know Marine jargon?"

"I am Sergeant Jim Stanton, Lima Co Third Battalion Fifth Marines."

"Well boys, I think we have found our insurgents," said Captain McGee. All of the men that had their weapons pointed at the Marines clicked off the safeties. "Hold on now boys, we were sent into this sector to help. Lower your weapons," he said, and the Marines did.

"Okay," said Jim, "Now you guys. What do you mean you are here to help?" asked Jim.

"We kept getting info over the U.N. net that a small group of locals were attacking convoys in this area and it was escalating. I'm sorry we didn't get here sooner to help in your ambush," said McGee. "We had it under control until the attack helicopters came into the picture and we realized that we had been set up."

"It could have been worse," said Jim. "If not for most of us being trained by Uncle Sam and of course having the advantage."

"Roger that," said the Captain.

"Not that I don't trust you Sir, but after today and what we have been through we need verification before we bring you up to speed and into our house."

"I thought you might say that, so I brought proof." A Marine brought out a laptop computer and opened it up. Captain McGee pulled up a video from his commanding officer, General Hummel, detailing what needed to happen to recover America. He showed the militia news footage of the initial attack that crippled America.

"Very few military commanders obeyed the unconstitutional order given by the President. We flew back from Afghanistan along with many other units from all branches to take our country back. For now, we have air support in this area and have established lines from which to push forward. We were not the only unit to parachute in. We have gotten word of successful attacks on many U.N. installations in this area. I can't guarantee things will get better right away, but for now you have the full support of the U.S. Military."

None of the men could believe what they were hearing. *Could things be over this fast?* Thought Jim.

"Captain, we need to get going to treat the wounded."

"Of course, we will accompany you and help however we can. I have a Navy corpsman if you can use him."

"We have a doctor," said Jim. "But more medical hands would be great."

"One more thing," said Captain McGee. "We have a C130 in orbit with food, water and medical supplies. He just needs a grid and he can drop the payload." Not knowing yet if they could be trusted, Jim gave him coordinates for two miles north of the cave. The supplies would be fine over the mountain, but if they were bombs or if the C-130 was a Specter Gunship they would just tear up wilderness.

The Marines took point, flanks and the militia's six hand in hand with the resistance fighters. They had hoped to bring trucks and supplies back this time, but since all were destroyed they had a few miles to walk.

They got to the outer perimeter after dark so Rick halted the combat patrol to confirm entry. He squelched his radio three times and saw two flashes of IR light in response. Everyone got into a single file line to avoid the traps. They made their way up the mountain to the stronghold of the cave system. Captain McGee mentioned to Jim on the way through the perimeter that it looked like they had their act together. Doc was called to attend to the wounded and the Navy corpsman helped. They put the dead under tarps just outside to be buried in the morning."Get some food and rest men," Jim said. "We will all meet for burial services for the fallen at eight a.m. Captain, these are our living quarters. We still need to talk further. Your men can stay in the main cave area until we can make other arrangements."

"I would like to volunteer them to help with perimeter security, if that would be alright."

"Not tonight," said Jim. "You and your men can stay right here if you don't mind. We will talk after we bury our fallen, I still have questions." The Marine captain did as he was asked. The men on watch were given explicit instructions to report anything out of the ordinary and to sound the alarm if the Marines tried to leave or wander into the cave further.

The next morning, everyone met in the main cave area to honor the men that had been lost. Make shift coffins were made with plywood. After a prayer and condolences were afforded to the families, the militia buried the men in a small graveyard south of the cave just outside of the perimeter.

"Captain, can you assemble your men, please?" asked Jim. "We all need to know everything."

Chapter Twelve: Common Ground

A meeting in the commons was set up for everyone to hear. Marine Captain McGee was more than forthcoming with information. He started at the beginning when the U.N. troops first entered the country.

"At first, they looked just like the U.N. troops we have all seen practicing on our bases. Then the amount of them began to raise concern in many places. Before we really knew what was happening, martial law had been implemented. With U.N. troops on all military bases, it was difficult to know where to start. They took over sea ports, airports and with the mixed troops on the bases no one wanted to start shooting. Here in Alaska, troops were sent to all cities and most rural areas. Six troop transports were flown in to the oilfield to take control of the pipeline on the North Slope in Prudhoe Bay. No shots were fired up there that we know of and with all the flammables, you can't blame them. Control of Valdez and its port gave them complete control of the oil supply. So far, no U.S. Military units have tried to take the pipeline or oilfield back. With thousands of people stranded up there, we have no idea when we will be able to get to them. The U.N. knows their expertise is needed to keep the oil flowing, so I'm sure they will be treated well enough to continue working for them. All of this information was retrieved from satellite images before we were shut out of our own systems.

"The idea behind this attack was to take over without firing a shot. At first it was working, but then militias formed, as well as rogue U.S. Military units fighting back. I'm sure this was to be expected and with U.N.'s air superiority, there was not much people could do to fight back. What made things clear for us was being overseas and then being re-deployed somewhere over here in the U.S. That is why it has taken a few months to get up here. Once we got everything figured out over there, we had to figure out where to strike here," said the captain.

"We want our country back too, but at what cost? Precision strikes were what had to happen in order to minimize civilian casualties. We have different units striking in different parts of the country. The problem is, there are over one hundred and fifty nations involved in this one world unity crap. Not all countries or citizens are on board, of course."

Bill, being the most knowledgeable on the one world power conspiracies, mentioned an article. He said, "I read about a James Paul Warburg, some foreign agent of the Rothchild Dynasty, he was a major player in the Federal Reserve Act scam. He made a statement before the U.S. Senate. 'We shall have world government, whether or not we like it. The only question is whether world government will be achieved by conquest or by consent.'"

"Sounds about right," said Jim. "I suppose we have our answer. The damn arrogant politicians were ready to just hand it all over, but we sure as hell aren't."

"Does anyone have any questions?" asked Captain McGee.

"So, is anyone on our side?" asked a voice from the back.

"Unfortunately, none that we are aware of," said McGee. "China is one of the major opposition players. The security council figured that once the U.S. fell off the world map then they would follow suit. They would rather see the U.S. stay as is since they have gotten rich off of us. They have sent in as many supplies as possible, but they are fighting a three front battle much like we are. Will they come to our aid after they have control back? We just don't know. This is a pretty conventional war. With so many countries involved in World War Three, no one will use a nuke. The worst that has happened is EMPs being set off, like the one that was used on Anchorage."

"So, we just continue on fighting until someone wins?" asked Jim.

"Pretty much," Captain McGee said with a sigh.

"And how do we know when that happens? If the U.S. Military does get the job done and gets rid of these invaders, what is stopping them from taking over?" asked a woman.

"The plan is to get the country back together and then start from anew. The Constitution is solid. It's the lazy, rich politicians that are the problem. We will start over, things will be better, but we have to make sacrifices before they will. Martial law will more than likely need to be implemented for a short time until order is restored," said McGee. "Not many people will like that answer, but that's how it needs to be and the people will deal with it like they did everything else."

"Thank you all and God bless," said Jim. "Please get back to what you need to do today. Captain, please come with me." Jim took McGee to a side room to talk. "So, how long will you be staying?"

"As long as we can," said McGee. "We will eventually be called out to another part of the country. We will do whatever you need us to do here while we can. By the way sergeant, did your people find the air drop?"

"We had it dropped on the other side of the mountain just in case it wasn't what you said it was."

"Fair enough, would you like the tracker for the electronic beacon attached to each package?"

"Why don't we just go get them together?" asked Jim.

"I will have my men combat ready in five minutes."

"Roger that," said Jim.

A patrol was put together with four wheelers and trailers. Half of the marines stayed back with Rick so he could go over security with them and fit them into a rotation on the perimeter.

They followed the beacon to the closest drop package. It was all intact and as they opened it, saw that it was a mixture of food and water. They loaded everything on the four wheelers and went back to the cave to drop it all off. Two Marines escorted them. The rest of the men went on to the second signal. When it was in sight, everyone was told to halt by the point man's hand in the air. They all took a knee and froze. The pallet of supplies was being torn apart by three people. "What do you want to do, Jim?" asked Captain McGee.

"Let me go down there and talk to them," he said. "Cover me from here; I'll squelch the radio twice if I need you to take them out." With a wave from his hand, Captain McGee had Marines fan out and take aim on the looters.

Jim walked slowly down to the air drop. When he got within a hundred yards or so he said, "Hello there." Rifles were instantly raised and pointed at him. "Easy now guys, I just want to talk." He kept walking toward them and was told to stop about twenty yards out.

"What do you want?" asked one of the men.

"I just want to see if I can have some of my stuff. I will share it with you," said Jim, "But I don't want you to take it all."

"This stuff fell out of the sky and no one was here to claim it."

"Well, we had to find it first with this." Jim showed them the tracker. "I will show you how it works so you can see that this is in fact mine."

"What's stopping us from killing you and taking it all?" asked the woman in the group.

"If I may show you, this is what will stop you." Jim took a water bottle out of the shipment, put it on a stump, and said, "Can you please make this go away?"

Jim had been talking on his radio. One of the Marine snipers with a silencer shot the bottle and it exploded. This put the people on edge and they raised their rifles at Jim again. "You need to lower you rifles, or you might be next." They did as Jim asked. The rest of the patrol walked down to meet them except for one Marine on over watch. "Now," said Jim. "What are you doing out here?"

The three people, two men and a woman, had been up at their cabin when everything started. There were five of them on a weekend getaway when they began and now were down to three. They left the cabin in search of food after being ambushed by U.N. troops, and left with what they carried. The woman lost her husband and one of the men lost his wife. After hearing their story, and in turn telling them about the Marines dropping in, they offered them safe haven. The desperate people of course were more than happy to join the group. The four wheelers found the patrol again. They were loaded up and sent back with the new people.

They had three more drop packages to find and half the day left to get them back. They continued on following the tracker. All packages were found and they were all back just after dark with enough food, water and medical supplies for another few months.

Chapter Thirteen: Trouble on the Home Front

With supplies abundant for now, everyone was happy...or so everyone thought. A family that had come to the mountain from town to escape the invaders was having problems. The oldest daughter had been seeing one of the Marines that had recently come to live on the mountain, and the father didn't approve, though the girl was nineteen. Tensions were rising and causing problems with security. The daughter, Millie, was sneaking to the Marine's post at night. This meant his watch partner had to leave in order to give them privacy. Not a good thing at all when you have so many lives at stake, not to mention an unhappy father. Jim could sympathize with the man; he had a daughter about the same age, named Alexis. His daughter was on the other side of the mountain with the original families that had come up and was out of harm's way for now. The Marine was not going to be on the mountain permanently and he was not being respectful of the father's wishes.

Captain McGee had to be brought in to stop this and to reprimand the Marine. A meeting was set between Jim, Captain McGee and Stan, the father of the girl.

The Marine, Sergeant Collins, was a good Marine and had lost a lot like most of the people. He said that he had been honorable and had not slept with Millie. He was falling in love with her. He wanted to stay to help the militia in its efforts when the Marines pulled out.

Captain McGee had already considered leaving two Marines back to help. Collins was not on the short list, not because he was a bad Marine. Stan would have the final say to whether Sergeant Collins would stay. "He has to earn my trust back," said Stan. "I believe in rebuilding this nation and this would be a good start, but my little girl is not going to just be a snack, she will be the whole meal and nothing else."

The decision was made to let Collins stay, as long as he did everything Stan required of him where his daughter was concerned. Captain McGee made it clear that Sergeant Collins was now under Jim's command, and that he also still had a duty to defend the country.

Why couldn't things be easy? Jim thought to himself. Just last week, Mary had gotten on to him about the boys and how they wouldn't clean up after themselves. "You just got to keep on them and teach them the best you can," he told her.

"Just because the world is turned upside down doesn't mean they can do whatever they want," she said.

"They were like this when it was right side up," said Jim. Rick's son, Eric, was getting better after being shot, but he was lazy at times, too. "Just because you got shot doesn't mean you can start slacking," he told Eric.

This was normal life mixed in with an abnormal one. "Everyone here is living pretty damn well considering everything," Jim kept telling everyone. Everyday life continued the best it could under the circumstances.

Every once in a while, they caught a thief and it was usually a kid. Times were tough, but you have to put forth effort to help out in order to receive help yourself, Jim always said. Punishments were handed out according to the crime. The young people had to be kept busy with chores. They no longer had the luxuries of the electronics they had grown up with. Hard work was good for them. The younger, softer generations needed more incentive to keep this country from falling to a more aggressive force.

These were minor issues compared to what was happening outside, but they all had to be dealt with. They had no idea how long this war would last. Throughout history most wars had lasted for a decade or more. The question was, could they last that long?

Chapter Fourteen: On the Offensive

After reviewing the information, Captain McGee and Jim came to the conclusion that the militia's U.N. contact must have been compromised. For now, they had the intel from the U.S. Military to work with. The might of the U.S. forces was stretched so thin that civilians were called up on a regular basis to help fight by recon elements before an invasion commenced. McGee knew that he didn't have to enlist these men because they were already in the fight.

The Marines helped out upgrading the winter fighting positions. The recon Marine was trained to hide and gather intelligence, so camouflaging an area came naturally to them. Everyone could tell that they were growing restless and as spring approached they went on more patrols. They were gone for days at a time. They never reported any enemy contact, but always came back with some kind of animal to eat. The snow slowly melted away and more people ventured outside.

As the months went by, summer was soon upon them. Mary, Jim's wife, and many other women and older children had been hard at work on the garden so they'd have fresh vegetables. The lines had pretty much

stabilized and not much fighting occurred in the immediate area. Fruit was a main concern and the people of
the compound had to travel greater distances to get the
nourishment that was needed to survive. They were of
course accompanied by militia and sometimes by Marines. There was plenty to trade with. Doc had given
instructions on the proper types of food that everyone
needed to stay in good health.

"Just because you're not on a boat, doesn't mean
you can't get scurvy," he told them on a regular basis.
"You need fruit as well as all that meat," he would say
when he saw a moose being cut up.

The summer gave more opportunity for everyone
to enjoy Alaska and with the fighting pretty much silenced, it could be enjoyed even more.

A mixed militia and Marine patrol walked up
through the perimeter one afternoon carrying a Marine in a make-shift litter. The sentry at the bottom of
the mountain alerted Jim on the radio.

"I am on my way," said Jim. He went to get Captain McGee who was on his way to meet Jim.

"I've already heard," said McGee. "Do you know
what happened?"

"Not yet," he said, as they walked out of the cave
entrance to meet the patrol. As the patrol got closer,
Captain McGee asked them what happened. The Marine had been shot by a civilian who thought they were
U.N. troops. The Marines captured the boy and questioned him before letting him go. They did not tell him
exactly who they were just in case the U.N. was in the

area. The boy would tell them and a search would be initiated.

By the end of August, salmon had been harvested from local rivers and the winter food stores looked good. Sporadic air drops of supplies made their way to them. What was requested was not always what was dropped, but with the Marines with them it really helped. They had made a lot of progress on the entire cave system and perimeter. With the Marines' help and their tactical knowledge, the perimeter was built better than they could have imagined. The tunnels connecting the guard posts would help protect them in the winter and help conceal their position from above. The cave system construction went faster with the extra help and Captain McGee wanted to keep his troops in shape, so it worked out for everyone. The fight was not over and everyone knew it.

One day a Marine came running into the main cave, desperately looking for Captain McGee. He had just heard over their secure net that the U.N. had launched a new national offensive. The Marines had been called to fight in Anchorage. The militia was asked to join the unit for the campaign to rid the city of U.N. forces. They had air superiority and the militia knew the urban fighting would be dangerous, but offered their assistance anyway. The Marines had been there for them when they needed them and the country needed them now. For some this was to be a first, and for others, it was back in the saddle again.

A plane was reported early the next morning with a chute deployed from it. An air drop wasn't scheduled to come in; this was a special one requested by Captain McGee. He had asked for uniforms, body armor, weapons and ammo. The latest night vision and thermal imaging was among the drop as well.

Eighteen men from the mountain were to go with the marines while two of the military men were to stay behind to help defend the mountain. Sergeant Collins was one of the two staying back, as well as Private Sanderson.

Two CH 53 Super Stallion helicopters approached and landed just outside the perimeter after orange smoke popped. The men said their goodbyes to their loved ones, loaded up on the helicopters and departed for the city. They were to join more Marine forces in a staging area just outside of Anchorage. The forward operating base was being protected by artillery and air support from fixed wing and rotary aircraft. On the way, they could see the small towns which looked beat up from all of the fighting. Buildings had been destroyed and you could still see smoke in certain areas.

"The push from friendly forces unfortunately damaged some of the structures along the way," McGee said to Jim over the com as they looked down below. They arrived about an hour later and landed on what looked like a football field. After the helicopters landed, they made their way off the birds and into the staging area.

They had the same uniforms as the marines except they had put red arm bands on to show that they were militia. As they walked through the platoons of Marines, they heard some of them commenting about how they shouldn't be wearing their uniforms. Jim approached a few Marines that were pointing and laughing.

"What is the problem, lance corporal?" asked Jim.

"Nothing, pops, just don't think you and the seven dwarfs belong here is all."

Jim knocked him on his ass with a single punch. Marines and militia were yelling at each other. Jim was on top of the kid. The commotion was stopped by a Marine major. Jim picked the young Marine up and asked him how old he was.

"I'm nineteen," he said.

"Listen up!" said Jim. "I am Sergeant Jim Stanton Lima Co 3/5. I have been off active duty for some time, but I haven't forgotten my place. This great nation needs us, all of us." Jim stared at the young Marine. "We are here to help fight for our freedom. Many of us are prior military, others have been properly trained. Don't ever underestimate the will to be free, boy." With that, they caught up with the Recon Marines. The major that started to break things up came over to apologize for the young Marine.

"No need to, sir," said Jim. "I have kids about his age and know how to deal with them."

"We are glad to have you here, Devil Dog."

"Glad to be here, sir."

"You were in 3/5 huh, how long ago?"

"About twenty years now," said Jim.

"A ten hut!" said a loud voice.

"At ease!" said another loud voice. "I am General Taft and we are here today to take back another American city!" The Marines roared. "We have little time before the attack, so get with your unit leaders for your tasking." With that, the Marines formed up into small groups to find out what areas of the city they would go to.

The militia was to fast rope in with the Recon Marines and provided security while they gathered intel. Their objective was the port. They needed to see if any ships were still full of supplies for the U.N. It didn't sound like much, but if they encountered troops it would get real interesting real fast.

The helicopter pilots took them in hard, low and fast into the landing zone. They stopped and hovered. Two teams roped in on either side of the docks to provide support for each other. Two snipers dropped in separately to provide over watch.

They encountered a small amount of resistance on the way into the facility. Sniper cover eliminated the threats before the team reached them. They were on their own inside, but the snipers would continue to provide security as they went in. The cargo office was what they needed to find. They cleared each room on their way upstairs. There was no one inside so far.

After reaching the cargo office, the Marines went to work looking through the files. "What exactly are we looking for?" asked Jim.

"Bills of lading," said a Marine.

"For what?" asked Jim.

"Please just cover us as we do our job, sir," he said.

Something was wrong. The hairs on Jim's neck stood up, he had a bad feeling. Gunfire erupted outside and the windows by the file cabinets came apart as bullets hit them. "This is Sierra two, we have heavy incoming. U.N. troops are dropping on top of the building and in the yard. We will cover your withdrawal as best we can, out."

"Downstairs everyone," yelled a Marine. The men covered each other to the door leading outside. "Sierra two, we are ready to exfil!"

"Go, go, go!" said the snipers over the radio. They left the building and moved between cover.

"This way," said a Marine. They followed him onto a ship docked nearby. "Okay, we need security teams to guard this door. You two men, with me," said the Marine. Jim followed two Marines into the back of the ship along with another militia member.

"Alright, now you got to tell me why we are really here!" demanded Jim.

"This ship has an EMP pulse weapon aboard and we are here to destroy it."

"Let's get to it then, Marine!" said Jim. The U.N. had left this place lightly guarded because they figured they wouldn't need it anymore. They had won and

America would join the rest of the newly formed World Government, or so they thought.

"Okay, here it is. This charge is ready to go; we have two minutes to get off the ship," said the Marine. "It's set, now let's move!"

They got off the ship with seconds to spare. The detonation was meant to do two things. Blow up the weapon and sink the ship. As they were exiting the ship, one of the Recon Marines was shot and fell to the ground. If they didn't leave the blast area, they would be incinerated. The other Recon Marine went back to help just as the explosion started. Jim looked back as bullets went flying by his head with loud snaps and whirrs. The two Marines were blown back onto the pier and were obviously killed by the explosion.

The snipers and ground troops made quick work of the U.N. troops. The remaining troops left the area. Jim walked over to what was left of the two Marines and took their dog tags off from around their necks. "You won't be forgotten brothers," said Jim.

"Mike, Uniform three, this is Phantom, over," came a voice across the net.

"This is Mike Uniform three; go ahead with your traffic, over."

"Move southeast to hook up with Mike, uniform two for building search, over."

"Roger that Phantom, out."

"Everyone, listen up," said a Marine Lieutenant. "We have been tasked with searching house to house.

We will meet our sister unit and move in conjunction with them."

"What about the KIA?" asked Jim.

We will mark their bodies with strobes and come back for them. "Here are their dog tags," said Jim as he handed them to the Lieutenant.

The snipers stayed back covering their six and would follow them as they made their way up the street. The attack force turned patrol was spread out enough so if they came under attack, casualties would be limited as they engaged.

"Where are all the people?" asked Sam. He was one of the guys that volunteered to come with them from the mountain.

The U.N. ran most of them out of town. The others were either rounded up or killed when they resisted," said a Marine.

They moved parallel to the other Marine unit down the street and soon entered the first of many buildings. The fighting raged on for the better part of a week. They encountered U.N. troops as well as civilians. The fighting was intense in some areas where larger concentrations of U.N. troops remained. The civilians were directed to a safe area near the arena. Air support was called in when needed and M1 Abrams tanks accompanied most patrols as they fought their way through the city. After what seemed to last forever, word came down that they had taken the city back and ruled the skies completely.

As the troops all moved back to the FOB, civilians were directed to re-enter the city. General Taft thanked the Marines and militia for their sacrifices. Very few Marines or militia were killed in the week of fighting, but the enemy lost thousands. The ones that weren't killed or wounded were defeated mentally. With no support or resupply, the remaining U.N. troops surrendered very quickly.

All combat troops were directed back to the FOB by command. The surveillance planes continued to fly over the city to make sure no more U.N. troops were hiding.

"Marines, we have been requested to help out Portland," said the general. "Team leaders have your Marines check their weapons and gear. Resupply and get ready to move."

Transport back to the mountain was arranged and gladly accepted. The militia loaded aboard helicopters the next day for the trip south. Parts of Anchorage were left in ruins. The campaign goal was to rid the city of U.N. forces and to try to leave the city intact if at all possible. This was accomplished for the most part. The city could be rebuilt, but the invaders had to be dealt with and were.

The militia flew back to the mountain, exhausted after the campaign. Everyone was in good spirits as the helicopters approached the landing zone. A hot shower and hot meal sounded real good, along with plenty of sleep.

After being dropped off, they gave thanks to the Marines and said goodbye. A patrol from the mountain met them at the bottom to help with anything they might need, Bill among them. They watched the helicopters fly away. Just before they were out of sight, one of them blew up, and the other was hit with rocket fire. The remaining helicopter limped away and disappeared.

"What the hell is going on, Jim?" asked Bill frantically.

"I don't know, but it can't be good." About three hours passed and a call on an encrypted frequency came in.

"Jim, this is Captain McGee, are you there?" Jessie quickly went to get Jim.

"I'm here Ccaptain, what is going on out there?"

"The U.N. launched a massive counter attack and we are losing momentum and our lines. We need you and your men to be ready. I will be in touch, McGee out."

"What about the request for them to go to Oregon?" asked Matt.

"Let's just hope they finish the job here before they leave us," said Jim.

Chapter Fifteen: Reengaged

The thought of losing what had been gained, especially after so much sacrifice, was sickening. The U.N., with hundreds of thousands of troops had not given up; in fact they came back with a fist of fury.

Jim and the families depending on him had hoped the nightmare was over, but the people behind the One World Government were relentless. Only one of the men that left to help the Marines had been wounded, and none died that week.

Winter would soon be on the way once again and they still had preparations to make. There had been no word from the contact within the U.N. since they were set up. A new contact had to be made in order to get the information they needed on convoys and troop strength. The group considered setting up a small base in town, but that would put more people at risk on a full time basis. This was brought up in one of the meetings with the populace of the stronghold. A man and his wife volunteered. "We feel that we have not helped as much as we could have until this point. This will be our contribution to our country," they said.

A safe house was set up in town for the couple to run things out of. A secret safe room was constructed so anyone would have a hard time finding it.

The couple, Dave and Sara Whitlock, would recruit new people for the cause and store weapons and supplies until they could be transported. So things didn't look suspicious, the safe house was set up in their old house. It was off the beaten path of the main highway and was easily accessed by the four wheeler trails that everyone had become so fond of.

The militia continued to use the radios the Marines had given them that were set up with encryption. The last thing they needed was to let the U.N. know where they were.

Everyone worked as fast as they could to get everything in place for the safe house before winter. A system was put in place for the Whitlocks to recruit more people and to get supplies that would be sent up to the cave compound. They had to be careful, but the movement had to go on. Eventually they would have the country back.

As November rolled around and the snow piled up, they wondered if the U.S. troops would come back to help them. Most of Alaska had been won back and then suddenly lost again. New troops from countries no one had ever heard of were controlling the convoys. The intel they were getting was that the troops they were now fighting were considered the New World Order. Rumors of different names for the world army could be heard everywhere.

December brought in warmer weather than expected, so ambushes could still happen with little effort using the infrastructure that was in place. The Alaskan

Militia was growing and everyone wanted the U.N. out of the country. As the month went on, the weather got colder, but the militia just adapted as it always had.

One cold day in early January, an ambush was set up on a small supply convoy. The militia had light snow and great cover. This was a routine ambush and was treated as one. Snipers were in position when the U.N. vehicles approached, and started to engage turret gunners when the claymore took out the lead vehicle. Troops in tan uniforms and black helmets came out of the vehicles and fought with a vengeance. They took them down, but this was a different style of fighting than they had seen with previous U.N. forces. As they mopped up and started to collect weapons, ammo and supplies, Terry said, "Hey Jim, come over here."

"What is it?" asked Jim.

"Look at the uniforms," said Terry. They were of course soaked in blood, but the shoulder patches were what were interesting. A scene of the earth with continents and three letters on top, NWA it read.

"What the hell is NWA?" Terry asked. He cut a patch off of one of the uniforms and brought it with them. "Look for any paperwork as well in the vehicles," said Jim.

"Two minutes people," said Jim. With that, everyone finished collecting what they could and made for the trees.

When they got back to the compound, Jim and Terry made their way through the cave system to the other side. This was restricted access due to potential cave-ins, a sign said. A steel door was put in the tunnel with security cameras posted on both sides. The existence of the other side of the tunnel was well guarded by the original inhabitants. They needed to keep their families safe and they really didn't know who could be truly trusted on the other side.

Once back at the cabin, they made a search for the meaning of the patch on the secure server. The results were not surprising. The search revealed, "New World Army."

"Does this mean we're losing?" asked Terry.

"That's exactly what they want," said Jim. "By putting the U.N. troops in these uniforms, they are demoralizing the populace."

"This website shows what they say has been converted. Looks like most of the world," said Bill. "China and the U.S. are mainly under the control of the world army according to this."

"I don't believe it!" said Jim. "We will just keep fighting and see this through to the end."

They got word from Dave and Sara in town that there was an important person on the way. Even with encryption, they wouldn't elaborate. A patrol was sent to the furthest outpost on the perimeter to bring back the mystery guest. The patrol got back just before dark with their friend from the U.N., Mike.

"Well, we thought you were dead, buddy!" said Rick.

"Where the hell have you been?" asked Jim.

"I was compromised, and barely escaped with my life. The men I worked under started an investigation and interrogated all the men that had access to vital troop movements. Somehow, and I still can't figure out how, they found me out. I was tipped off just before I walked into a trap," said Mike. "I was in Anchorage and had to sneak my way back."

"Well. I'm glad you got word before, would have been nice if we had!" yelled Rick. "We lost men on that ambush that you said was a soft target."

"You do know we are taking one hell of a risk by having you here, don't you?" asked Matt.

"I know and I don't want to put you in danger, but I have information you will want to hear..."

They set up a video camera and Mike started talking. What he had to say made a lot of sense, but was it the truth? The New World Army was put together by the U.N. because it was losing. They started the website everyone saw and put all U.N. troops in the new uniforms. The troops were given false hope and information in order to lift their spirits and willingness to fight. The reason it looked like they had taken back over is that the NWA was stretched too thin. They were deployed in small units all over the world. The world resistance was much more than was anticipated. Government politicians had given their countries over to the U.N. for money and power no doubt, but the troops had other plans. Not only military forces resisted, but civilians as well.

"You are not the only pocket of resistance," said Mike. "It is just a matter of time before the NWA is taken out of the picture."

They sent Mike away with an armed escort. As a collective, they needed to talk about the new information that had been given to them. A meeting for the leaders of each group that had come to the mountain to help fight was scheduled for the morning.

Chapter Sixteen: The Assassin

As if things were not bad enough, a man on close perimeter security was found with his throat cut in the early morning hours by his relief. An immediate investigation was launched first thing in the morning.

"What do you think, Jim?" asked Rick.

"I think we have a problem," Jim answered. "The furthest perimeter outposts said there was no sign of someone slipping through. Between the guard shacks, the traps and the trenches no one could get in here. They either parachuted in or we have an internal issue."

"Did anyone check on our U.N. spy?" asked Rick.

"Mike was guarded all night by two men," Jim said.

"That was the first thing that went through my mind," said Rick.

"Keep him guarded anyway. He is an asset we want to hold on to. He will have to stay in his room until this is figured out."

"Matt, you're the closest thing to law enforcement we have. Would you mind taking charge here and figuring out who did this?" asked Jim.

"I'll get right on it. I don't want anyone to go anywhere alone until we have caught the person responsible."

They had a community meeting and told everyone, no matter what they did or where they went, to have at least one or more persons with them. People were demanding guns to protect themselves, and asking how this could have happened. Jim spoke up.

"We have properly trained personnel that carry firearms. The last thing we need is for someone to get shot because you thought he or she was going to hurt you. Listen people, we have all lived together for months, and some more than a year. This has to be someone that has infiltrated the compound. We will find the perpetrator. Please, just cooperate with Matt Woods here. He is in charge of the investigation."

People were uneasy and with good cause. Security on the perimeter was doubled as was internal security. Jessie installed the few remaining cameras she had left in vital areas and put in a request for more from town.

The next morning, most woke to screaming. A posted militia member was found just outside the cave entrance with his throat cut. The man that was on post with him was nowhere to be found. They searched half the day for him. He was finally found outside the perimeter, having suffered the same fate. None of the men had any weapons or personal belongings taken. "How the hell did he get outside our perimeter?" asked Matt.

"Matt, you keep up the investigation. Rick, you and the rest of the troops are now on high alert. I am taking Terry with me to town to get cameras even if we have to steal them," said Jim. "No one is to leave or enter besides us. I want restricted movements inside and out. Pull everyone back from perimeter security to the cave entrance after setting booby traps with flares attached. Terry and I will take the north exit from the cabin side. Everyone is to be accounted for at all times."

The trip wires were set as they made their way up the mountain. "Jessie, I want someone to be posted on these screens at all times, no exceptions," said Jim. "Terry and I are going to town to get you more cameras."

"I'll need more screens too," she said.

"We'll get them." Jim and Terry got on their sleds and headed to town.

Jessie watched as the two men passed the western most surveillance camera. "I hope they hurry..." she said to Bill.

"We know it's no one on this side of the mountain," he said. "But will the murderer stay away?"

"As far as anyone here knows, nobody else knows about this side," she said.

"They've got to wonder why the door is in the middle of the tunnel," said Bill.

"Why would they question it?" she asked. "We've taken care of all of them for this long."

"Things change," said Bill.

Matt and Rick were busy setting up what they hoped would be the next target. Everyone had been pulled back to the cave and most were in their rooms.

They positioned snipers with thermal and night vision in the main cave. Rick was on tunnel security by the restricted door leading to the other side with a guy that had been with the group for about two months.

At four a.m. men rotated shifts at the cave entrance. Rick pretended to go to sleep at his post. "Okay, he is coming up behind you now, just let it happen." Jim had returned at about midnight and infiltrated the perimeter just outside the cave entrance. He slipped past the sentries on post; he'd deal with them later. "If this is the guy then he will be on you any second."

Rick felt his head being pulled back and a knife across his throat. He slumped down in the chair and Jim took the shot. Rick bounced back to his feet and aimed his rifle at Dmitry. "Why?" Rick asked.

"For my world!" he yelled as he tried to cut his own throat, but Rick was too fast. He kicked the knife out of Dmitry's hand. Within seconds, six rifles pointed at Dmitry. "Take him to the holding cell," said Jim.

At breakfast that morning, Bill asked the men, "How did you know it was Dmitry?" Matt recounted the story for everyone. The serrations on Dmitry's knife was the main thing that gave him away, and his strength. Not many people could carry Jeff down the mountain and sneak through the perimeter. He had firsthand knowledge of all personnel, patrols and security procedure. He was good, but Matt was better.

"What will you do with him?" asked Jessie.

"We will interrogate him and get as much information out of him as we can before he faces the firing squad," Jim said. "He has committed treason and will pay the ultimate price."

"Let's get Mike back out there and see if he can generate any good information for us," Jim said to Matt.

"Sure thing, boss," said Matt.

Dmitry had to be tortured for days before he would give anything up, which wasn't much. He infiltrated the mountain primarily to cause internal chaos. The NWA knew where they were and would come for them before long, he said.

"Put everything and everyone back to standard security," Jim said. "We will still put up the new surveillance cameras and for now, no new people will be allowed to enter the compound. We will hold services for the three men as soon as the storm breaks and we can dig graves."

The winter raged on and, as usual, nearly everyone got cabin fever—or cave fever to be exact. Dmitry's arrival and his disruption in the compound kept everyone on edge for a while. They wanted to get out, since they had been confined to quarters more than usual. Jim relented and on a warm spring day, the women and children got to go outside and sled down a hill that the militia had made for the occasion. A number of snowmachines had been brought over to the hill to take the people back to the top for another ride down.

To protect everyone, a long range recon patrol was stationed miles from the mountain; they would alert the lower perimeter security stations of anything incoming.

"For the sake of morale, this had to happen," Jim said to Bill as they stood watching the fun.

"I agree with you whole heartedly," said Bill. "This is a good thing you've done."

Everyone had a great time during the much needed outing and continued to talk about it for days after.

Chapter Seventeen: Danger

It was getting close to two years since most people had left their homes for the mountain sanctuary. Summer was once again right around the corner. Planting seeds for crops, berry picking, and catching salmon when the runs came up the river were upcoming priorities.

Most people were getting restless and ready to enjoy some warm weather. The outpost in town had been quiet for a few days. They were about to send in a patrol because they couldn't get an answer to radio calls. They soon found out why.

Dave finally contacted them on the encrypted radio. He said that he needed the leaders to come to his house. They all knew what this meant. The enemy had found Dave and Sara. Rescuing their friends seemed unlikely, but they had to try.

A force of thirty-five militia members left the compound in the early morning hours the following day. They knew they were in for a fight and went as prepared as possible. Jessie was tasked with trying to get the Marines on a secure net to provide assistance. They wouldn't know if she got through unless they showed up.

With the help of the cover of darkness, night vision and thermal imaging, they were able to locate all the hidden NWA troops and position their own troops to take them out. They started on the perimeter and made their way toward the house. The men carefully entered the house through a secret underground passage that led them into the basement. The idea was to take the NWA by surprise.

As they entered the basement, the militia troops on the outside cut the power. They assaulted the house like trained experts. Dave and Sara were in the living room, tied down to chairs. When the troops approached, Dave told them to get back. They had been booby-trapped with explosives. "This is Alpha two," said Rick. "Get the lights on and get Steve in here. We need an explosives expert."

"I want everyone to stay alert," said Jim over the radio. "Keep night vision and thermal on. I want to know if anyone sees anything out of the ordinary."

The militia troops maintained a 360 degree perimeter around the house and spread out for two hundred yards. "Let's get these off of you," Steve told Dave and Sara. He went to work and removed the explosives within fifteen minutes.

"Grab whatever you need, we are leaving and not coming back," Jim told the couple.

"I'll help you," said Matt.

Just as they were leaving the house, the radio erupted with "Incoming troops!" A firefight lit up the perimeter all around them.

"Fall back, I say again fall back!" said Jim. All of the militia members fell back to the house.

"We are sitting ducks here," said Rick with frustration.

"Give me a staggered formation, move north!" said Jim. They encountered light resistance and soon found out why. All the NWA troops had pulled back because of the air strike that pounded the house just after they left.

"We got out of there just in time," said Dave. Everyone made their way to the sleds. Jim decided to stop, wait and listen to make sure they weren't followed a few miles away. After an hour, he was satisfied and they continued on. They made their way to the perimeter just before daylight, put the sleds in their bunkers and went into the compound to debrief their friends.

"What happened? Start from the beginning," said Bill.

"Sara and I were eating breakfast and there was a knock at the door. I opened the door to a NWA officer. This has happened before so I invited him in. He asked to see our World ID cards, which we gave him. 'I have heard rumors of a safe house and ties to insurgents,' he said. Right after he said that, troops came through both doors and cuffed us. 'We don't know what you are talking about,' I told him. He said he was sure he had the right house and that he'd find us out soon enough. I told him torturing us would be useless, that we'd say anything to make them stop. He said, 'Oh, we don't torture our own citizens, we just inject you with Sodium Pentothal and you tell us everything we want to know.'" Dave shook his head.

"We were then tied up in the chairs you found us in. Within an hour, Sara and I couldn't stop talking...I am so sorry guys..." said Dave.

"Not to worry," said Bill. "We have had closer calls and we are all glad to have you back and unharmed."

Dave and Sara were welcomed back into the little community that they had left to do their duty. They got a room to stay in that was close to their old one and were just happy to be back among friends again and out of harm's way.

Chapter Eighteen: Demoralized

With no contact in town now, they had to send out long range reconnaissance patrols. These LRRP teams consisted of four men. They were not to engage the enemy unless it was a small unit they could take out without collateral damage or compromising the mission. Each team had a sniper, machine gunner and two basic riflemen. Rick, Matt and Jim started a competition to see who could get the most confirmed kills. This all came about when Rick and his team were on a patrol for intel about a supply convoy that was headed their way. The patrol set up outside of a compound and watched it for two days. Satisfied they had enough evidence the convoy was on its way, they left the area and started heading back. An enemy patrol was spotted about one thousand yards away down a hill. There were five men, and Rick said, "We should take them out so they don't find the hide we were in." Rick set up his silenced semi auto sniper rifle. With cover from the rest of the squad, he shot the soldier in the front and then the one in the rear. The three in the middle were confused as they died seconds after the others.

As each team came in from their patrols, the score on the board grew larger. This was a morale boost for most in the compound. The mission had to be completed before the snipers could engage any size force. Sometimes the team had to find targets outside of the mission area in order to keep the snipers and the whole team in the running for the highest score. The rest of the team did back up the sniper, so the sniper didn't get credit for the kill unless he pulled the trigger. The scores were confirmed only by the other team members. The snipers had to be true to their word or it wouldn't work. The men all knew each other well which made it easier. The LRRPs started seeing signs, offering a reward for the name and whereabouts of any snipers. This made it all the more exciting. Not only were they killing the enemy and making things safer for the locals, they were bringing down the morale of the enemy.

Sometimes two shots to the body had to be fired at a target. This meant they had started using better body armor. The new competition was head shots. Many of the snipers' kills had been head shots, so those numbers were just added to that category and taken out of the body shot record.

Matt and his team encountered a small NWA patrol on one LRRP. "They seem undisciplined, carefree. Something isn't right here guys..." Rick said on his radio.

"They must be new guys, just take them out," replied Danny.

"Hold on Danny, give me a sweep of the area with thermal." It was daylight, but the thermal worked day or night.

"Hey, Rick!" said Danny more excited than usual. "We have hundreds of troops in the hills!" he said.

"Okay everyone, let's slowly move back to behind our hill and Danny, stay on the thermal as we fall back," said Rick. The four troops had been bait, locals dressed in NWA uniforms. This was confirmed by an enemy soldier captured a few days later by another patrol.

The group talked about it back in the cabin and decided that thermal would be used at all times during ops to try and make sure no one was compromised, and that the targets were legitimate.

The enemy was getting more aggressive and they had to be extra careful in order to avoid bringing them back to the mountain. They had been lucky with Dave and Sara's capture. Apparently, the information given to the NWA commander didn't get passed on. If it had, the mountain stronghold would have been bombed already.

Chapter Nineteen: Loneliness

Why am I here, why is it so dark? I can't hear anything. What the hell is going on?

I see another bright flash of light. Okay, I can see a little, but it's blurry. Hey, where am I? Hello, say something! Who's blood it that? Talk to me, damn it! You can't hear me, can you? My god, this isn't happening to me. Okay, I felt that! Ow! Stop that! Wait, what is in that needle? Doc, don't, no, no!

Jim's thoughts faded back into unconsciousness, unheard by those around him.

"How are you doing, Rick?"

"I'm better than Jim. I'm sorry Mary. I know Doc will do everything he can for him. Are you and the kids okay?" asked Rick.

"We'll be fine. Please, tell me what happened out there."

"We decided to hit a convoy full of troops. We were outnumbered five to one, but we had the advantage. This was what you would call a textbook ambush. We have all done this a hundred times. The attack started off just as planned until they got out of the armored personnel carriers, set up mortars and started to fire randomly. With all the suppressed weapons we have, they couldn't have seen all of us firing. The snipers are always at a further distance than the main force. We continued to engage as the mortars fell. It was an unlucky round that fired in Jim's direction. He didn't even know it was on the way. I don't think so anyway. He is lucky he had all of his body armor on or this could be much worse. I saw the explosion at his position and made my way over there as soon as the fighting would let me. As I approached the area, I saw a small crater from the mortar round and no Jim. I continued to look and I saw him crawling away through the alders. He collapsed and I called for assistance. We got him here as soon as we could, Mary."

The whole compound was praying for Jim. They had lost people before, but none would impact the collective like losing him. He had brought them together and kept them safe. None of them would have made it this far without him.

The surgery lasted four hours. "What can you tell us, Doc?" asked Matt.

"He is stable for now and I think I got most of the shrapnel out of him. He is very lucky to say the least."

Rick was second in command and would do his best in Jim's absence, but he would be glad to have their leader back on his feet.

The sniper competition was put on hold until Jim could get back out into the field. The mood was very different around the compound without him directing everyday business.

Four days after Jim was wounded, he regained consciousness. Everyone was told over the radio that he was awake. Mary and the kids were in the room when people started to arrive.

"Okay, calm down everyone," said Matt. "We will all get a chance to see him." Jim had bandages all over his right side. He still had all his limbs, except for his right pinky, which had been severed at the middle knuckle. Aside from that, he was in one piece.

"You have a lot of people to see you, honey," said Mary.

"Have Matt make a list for me and I will call for them a few at a time. They need to keep the compound running. Please tell them I am grateful for all they do," said Jim. With that, people started leaving.

"Doc, when can I leave this room and go home?"

"We will see how you're doing next week," he told Jim. "I don't want you tearing any stitches."

"Roger that," said Jim.

"Mary, I remember being brought into the operating room. I tried to talk to everyone, but no one could hear me. It was like a dream. I was yelling, but no noise came out."

"It was shock," said the doctor. "Your body shut down certain areas to start working on them. Your brain kept going. This sounds similar to what coma patients experience."

"Yeah, I couldn't handle it and then you gave me a shot."

"I put you under so I could remove all the shrapnel. If I had an x-ray machine, I could tell more but for now I think I got it all. Let me know if you experience pain or discomfort anywhere that is worse than you feel right now."

"Will do," said Jim.

"Now, get some rest and heal," he said.

Jim woke up a few hours later screaming. He'd had a nightmare.

"I remember."

"Remember what?" asked Mary. She hadn't left his side for long.

"The ambush and the mortars," he said. "I was taking out each mortar squad from the front of the convoy to the rear. As I put my cross hairs on the last one, it looked like they had found me. I got off five rounds and starting displacing when the world exploded around me. I crawled into some alders to avoid any other rounds heading my way. It's pretty hazy after that, until I got here."

The days turned into weeks. Jim was growing restless. He watched the compound's entire DVD library. Then it was time to start rehab. He got dressed and started walking through the tunnel toward the main cave area.

It was slow going, but he could see the smiles on everyone's faces. This made things easier for him. It hurt like hell, but he had to get back into shape and back in the fight. "Pain is just weakness leaving the body," he kept telling himself.

Jim walked into Rick. "Hey buddy," said Jim.

"What the hell are you doing up and about?"

"I came to get a sit rep from you." The two of them sat down at one of the eating tables and Rick told Jim everything that had happened in the last three weeks.

"The ambush was another set up," said Rick. "Good news is that we gained more machine guns for the perimeter and three of the four mortars are still operational. The trucks were loaded with ammo and mortar shells. We can defend this place really well now."

"As soon as I am feeling up to it, we are getting back out there in full force," said Jim.

"You got it," said Rick. "We've still been sending out patrols, but not much has been happening. I think we might have scared them off."

"Either that, or they're getting ready to attack us in force," said Jim. "Keep security tight and keep the patrols up to the same level. We don't need any surprises."

Chapter Twenty: A River Runs Through It

The kids had played hide and seek in the tunnels for months and no one had had any issues with it until the electricity went out.

A strong windstorm, stronger than they had ever seen, swept through the mountains and knocked over two of the windmills they had erected. The entire cave system relied on the windmills for power. Not just for lights, but for heat and humidity levels.

The storm lasted for three days. On the first evening, everyone got word that three kids were missing. A search party was organized.

"First, we need to start on one end of the tunnel system and work our way toward the main entrance," said Matt. "From there, we will work our way through the perimeter. I want all sentries to stay at their posts and let us handle this."

Matt was the resident law enforcement official. He had only been a corrections officer, but he was the best they had. He was the security officer as well.

The kids were supposed to have at least a flashlight with them, as was everyone, in case of emergencies. Danny was the one that found the door, which led to an off limits part of the system, unlocked. The ceiling and walls had not been reinforced enough for people to occupy this part.

The search party had not gone outside yet, so they decided to check the area beyond the door. Everyone in the search party filed through. The tunnel was very damp and got very loud the further they went in.

"The cave is flooding!" someone yelled.

"No," said Matt as he got closer. "It's an underground river and we are at the falls. Look down there," he yelled. They could barely make out a beach and a pool of water at the bottom.

"I think we can get down here," said one of the guys in the search party. The roar of the falls slowly dissipated as they made their way down toward the pool.

"Did you guys know this was here?" asked a man in the search party.

"It sure wasn't here last year," said Matt. "We must not have ventured this far into this tunnel for some reason. I thought we had explored and mapped out all of it."

"The tunnel keeps going up beyond the pool. We need to cross and go look," said a woman.

"I want you two to stay here, the rest of us are going to go back up to the main cave. We need to get rope, a small raft, more lights and floatation gear," said Matt.

"Why don't we just walk across?"

"Because," said Matt, "we don't know how deep it is or what the bottom is made of. I can tell you that the water is glacier run off and you would die of hypothermia within minutes if you went in."

Twenty minutes later, Matt and a few men returned with the equipment and got started. Meanwhile, in the main cave, word of a river a few hundred yards away, inside no less, made many people excited. The thought of not having to go into the cold and bring back snow to melt for drinking and cooking water was a godsend.

Matt shot an arrow with 550 cord attached into the wall on the other side. He set his bow down, climbed into the little rubber raft and pulled himself to the other side. After getting over, he secured a rope to an anchor and the men made a simple rope bridge. Four other men crossed to the other side to continue the search. The tunnel started to wind up and they could feel air on their faces after walking for about fifteen minutes. "Go slow..." said Matt. The men reached a large room and saw lights on the other side. "Lights out," said Matt quietly.

Lights pointed at them and they faintly heard people talking. The people made their way toward Matt and the others.

"Who are you?" asked Matt.

"We are the occupants of this cave, and who are you?" asked a woman.

"We lost three kids and came in here looking for them. We mean you no harm."

"Please come with us," she said.

They followed, but not too close. Matt could see the entrance of the cave with snow all around it.

"How is it so warm in here?" he asked.

"The hot spring over there near the opening has heated this place for as long as I can remember," she said. "My name is Kali."

"How many people are here?" asked Matt.

"Just the six of us," she said. "Three once you take your children. They wandered in here soaking wet two days ago." She pointed at a tent.

The men went over and called for the kids, who came right out. "We are so glad to see you!" they said. "The lights went out and we got lost and fell into the water."

"Everything is okay now. We are going to take you back to your parents. How long have you been here?" Matt asked Kali.

"We came up here to get away from the invaders last year."

Have you seen anyone else since?" asked Matt.

"No," she said.

Matt introduced himself and the rest of the men. "Would you like to come with us to the other side of the mountain, to our sanctuary?" The man, woman and child all looked at each other and then back at the men in disbelief. "I tell you what, come over and check it out and if you don't like it you can come back."

They agreed. "Would you like help with your belongings?"

"No," said the man. "We will decide if we want to stay once we have seen what you have to offer, and can come back."

The group made their way back into the belly of the mountain, back across the river and up to the main cave. Kali and her family couldn't believe their eyes. People gathered around to greet them. The kids that had been lost ran to their parents.

"This is our community. We have built it away from the NWA troops. You are welcome here," said Matt, as he motioned for a woman. "Jane, if they decide to stay can you show them to one of the newly constructed living areas please?" asked Matt.

"Will do," she said.

"Oh, and find out their skills and let Doc check them out."

We have a river right near us and the kids are safe. Life seems to be getting better, thought Matt.

Chapter Twenty-One: Sickness

A plan was put in place to bring electricity lines into the old tunnel, put up lights along it, and light up the area by the pool and river. The plumbers and carpenters combined their knowledge and resources to build a pump house, after stairs were built down to the pool.

They were bringing water to the common area with buckets from right down the tunnel for now, until a water line could be put in place. This was much more convenient already than bringing it in from outside.

The construction was underway and looking great. After a week of solid work, down there in the old tunnel and around the water, a few of the men started coughing. The Doc gave them regular cold medicine and told them to stay warm. A heater was already in the work area because of the colder temperature from the icy water running through. This was thought to be the problem until one of the plumbers started coughing up blood. The project was put on hold and the workers were quarantined so no one else would get sick. The area was closed off and water had to be brought in from outside again temporarily.

After three days, the men started getting better. "I think we need a look at the area they were working in," said Doc. Gas masks were donned and a few men went in to assist the doctor.

"What are we looking for?" asked Jim.

"I don't know just keep an eye out for anything unusual..." said Doc. The men looked for hours with lights at everything on their side, the pool area, and the other side without any luck.

Sam, an engineer and scientist that had offered to help because of his background was staring at the ceiling. They all slowly looked up and asked him what he was looking at. "The fungus on the rocks, it's glowing after you take the light away," he said.

"Ok," said Jim. "And...what does that mean?"

"I don't know, but do you see the particles falling in the light?" asked Sam.

"It just looks like dust," said Matt.

"It is dust, a certain kind of dust. I think the fungus is shooting out spores because it doesn't like the light."

"You mean like a defense mechanism?" asked Doc.

"Exactly," said Sam. "We need to take some samples and run some tests to make sure, but I think we found the reason those men got sick."

Without the right equipment they couldn't be certain, but this was the only answer they could come up with. No one had gotten sick from drinking the water and the men had only recently been around one another, other, other than just passing each other in the cave. A plan was put in place to tarp the ceiling where the fungus was so it stayed in darkness all the time. This would keep them from inhaling the spores.

A team went into the tunnel and river area to put the tarp up. Lights had to be used to see, so they wore masks again. A week was allotted for the spores to settle and hopefully not cause any more problems. No one had gotten sick before, because just passing through didn't give a person enough time to inhale many spores.

The construction continued and the bridge, pump house and new water system were up and running quickly. No one got sick again and they figured they had fixed the problem.

"That was an interesting one," Doc said to Bill once everything was back to normal.

"How do you mean?" asked Bill.

"Well, with combat wounds, the lack of proper food and supplies, and no one really getting sick with a cold or flu until this...I'm just saying that all it took was a fungus to stop things in their tracks and we have been at this what, two years now?"

"I know what you mean." said Bill. "We have had it pretty good..."

Chapter Twenty-Two: Normal

The snow was melting again and the compound was in full swing preparing for the coming summer. Plans were set in motion for getting outside and enjoying longer days and warmer weather. The repair to the windmills was a priority, they needed to have full power once again. Full patrols were watching the perimeter now that things were warming up. They had more people than ever. The community had grown to about one hundred people. Two school teachers had been teaching the kids throughout the winter, and soon it would be summer break for them. The future was uncertain, but they were going to live as normally as possible.

The back side of the mountain was chosen this year for growing crops. Kali, the woman whose family they ran into in the cave, told them with the tree cover and open fields it would be a good area to put the garden.

A permanent bridge had been built across the underground river and it became the escape route in case the mountain was overrun. Lights now went down the entire length of the tunnel and the pool of water was lit up as well. The pump station that had been built by the bridge had piping that ran all the way to the common area. There was a filter on the pump and at the spout on the other end. Some of the purest water most had ever tasted was now accessed underground. This freed people up to do other things, instead of bringing water inside from the outside stream or bringing in snow to melt and filter. More shower stalls were built and tanks set up for hot water. Creature comforts helped the morale and since no combat operations were ongoing at this time, it was a much needed benefit. A few people built a small getaway on the other side by the hot spring in their spare time. This became a vacation spot, and the reservation list filled up fast. More electricity had to be brought to that side, but it was worth it.

The other side of the mountain was a better hunting area too. More moose were taken from the area that summer and fall then they had killed the whole time they had been up there. They only took the game that they needed, but with more people the extra meat was necessary.

A cooler had to be constructed in order to keep the food longer. This was possible with the electricity from the windmills, and the people with technical skills made it happen. Berry picking was something that they had done from the beginning, but with more people, more berries could be picked. This made for an abundance of blueberries, salmonberries, cranberries and raspberries for pies, jams and many other things that added some fresh fruit to everyone's diets.

The recent recon patrols didn't have much to report. The NWA seemed to be nowhere. Jessie had been trying to get in touch with the Marines on the net all winter. She still tried every once in a while.

More and more young people wanted to join the militia and help the cause. Jim made a rule that you had to be eighteen to join and that women still would not fulfill combat rolls unless absolutely needed. There was of course opposition to this, but the young people were trained all the same. They needed to continue on with future generations of Americans and this could not be done if the women were killed in combat, but some didn't see it that way. Jim had healed from his injuries and was back to his normal self. He was glad to be back among the living.

A big meeting was called and everyone gathered in the main cave area. "We are putting together a small convoy to drive to the towns north of here," said Jim. "With little or no enemy activity in the last few weeks, we need to know what is happening. We still have no contact with the Marines. Any volunteers for the convoy please see Matt afterwards." A few grievances were brought up and would be taken care of. They had put together a nice little community amid all the violence.

The convoy of four vehicles left early the next morning. As the vehicles passed through each small town heading north, they saw people everywhere. Not many vehicles at all were on the road. This was a concern.

They got within ten miles of the Kenai River community of Soldotna and the lead vehicle stopped. "Checkpoint," came across the radio.

"Everyone stop, I want to turn around," said Jim. All the vehicles turned around and pulled off where the people at the checkpoint couldn't see them. "I want a four-man recon team to give me all the intel you can on our friends down there."

"I will take my team," Rick said. They took off through the woods. They would maintain radio silence unless they needed help.

"I want two snipers giving these boys cover," said Jim. "Crawl up to get into position and don't fire unless I tell you to. Take the Barrett .50 cals and spotters." Everyone knew what to do and did it without hesitation. The recon team, lead by Rick, slowly made its way through the woods to a position above the road in order to get a good look at the road block. An hour after the team had entered the woods they made their way back to the convoy.

"What can you tell us?" asked Jim.

"Well the road block has been set up by the NWA in order to keep track of civilian movements north and south. The soldiers are all kids. I walked right up to them," said Rick.

"You did what?" asked Jim.

"They aren't even armed," said Rick.

"So," asked Danny, "is it over? Can we go home?"

"No, they are still here. I don't care if they are kids and not armed," said Jim. "Something doesn't feel right." He looked around his surroundings and then back to his team. "I want a six man team with one vehicle to stay here with a secure radio. I want regular reports every two hours. Maintain fifty percent watch at all times. We need to get in touch with the Marines.

We will send supplies and relief in three days. Keep a low profile and watch your perimeter at all times," said Jim, who got back into his vehicle and started to drive back to the mountain.

Chapter Twenty-Three: Contact

The convoy made its way back to the stronghold before nightfall. Everyone was eager to hear the news, any news.

"Alright, everyone calm down,'" said Jim. "We encountered a roadblock about ten miles south of Soldotna, manned with young boys in NWA uniforms and no weapons." Everyone was talking at once. "If you want to find out, you have to let me talk people." They stopped talking again so Jim could tell them the rest. "So, Rick went to talk to them after seeing that they posed no threat. The boys were from Canada and they were just flown in to help the NWA with civilian reconstruction," they said. Everyone looked around with confusion. "I don't know what it means either. We are going to keep trying to get a hold of the Marines and get more info. In the meantime, we will be keeping an eye on the road block with a rotating team of six. The first team is in place and will be sending us regular reports. We will let all of you know what we find out just as soon as it happens. Sergeant Collins," said Jim.

"Yes sir," said the Marine.

"I need you to follow me son." The two men walked through the commons and down an old tunnel.

They went through the door marked, No Entry, Collapsed Tunnel.

"Sir?" asked Collins. "Where are we going?"

"Just follow me and keep quite." They turned their weapon lights on and skirted the wall by a huge hole in the tunnel floor. They turned a corner and could see lights further down the tunnel. Collins could see kids playing in the tunnel and many rooms alongside as they walked through to another door.

Jim opened the door and they walked into the cabin where several people were sitting around the main room. "This is Bill," said Jim. "He owns this cabin and this is our home away from home."

"I have heard much about you, Sergeant Collins, as have the rest of us. I asked you here to help our computer tech Jessie. I trust you will not say a word about this side to anyone?"

"No sir, you have my word," said Collins.

"Not even Millie can know."

"Yes sir."

"Come over here please," said Jessie.

They went into a room that was full of computers and communication equipment. "This is our command center. I need your help to get in touch with Captain McGee," said Jessie. "I have been trying all winter with no luck. Can you help us?"

"Before he left, Captain McGee gave me a frequency and code. He said to use it only in extreme emergencies."

"Who is on the other end?" asked Bill.

"He didn't say," said Collins.

"Jessie, put it in and let's see who we get," said Jim.

"We will have audio and video in ten seconds," she said.

"This is mobile command," said a voice, and a figure moved in front of the screen. "Who is this?"

"This is Jim Stanton of the Alaskan Militia in free America and who are you?"

"This is General Hummel, United States Marine Corps son. How did you get this frequency on my secure net?"

"Captain Daniel McGee of First Force Recon gave it to us. Can you give us a sitrep sir?" asked Jim. "We have been out of contact and need to know."

"What's the password?" asked the General.

"Chesty," said Collins.

Jessie looked confused.

Jim whispered, "I will tell you later."

"Good, now to business," said the General.

"Most of the West Coast has been secured and we are heading east. We still have resistance in the south, but have air superiority in most areas. How is it up there in Alaska?"

"We haven't had much resistance from the NWA," said Jim. "We encountered a small road block this morning with kids manning it, and no weapons. Do you have any intel for us about the rest of Alaska?"

"The last we heard is the NWA had taken control of the oil pipeline again and was moving more troops in to keep control. We unfortunately are stretched too thin with our forces to go back up there anytime soon. We have more civilians down here in other states to worry about. I'm sorry, but it has become a numbers game and you will just have to hold out as long as you can. We will be back up there just as soon as possible."

The image and sound were blinking out. "What happened?" asked Jim.

"The satellite has left the horizon. We can try again tomorrow," said Jessie.

"No need, we heard all we needed to hear," said Bill. "We are on our own and don't know when we can expect any help."

With that, Jim and Sergeant Collins left to go back to the other side of the mountain.

"What do you think, Jim?" asked Collins.

"Well, what the General said makes sense. The main population of the U.S. is a priority, but so is the oil up here."

"I don't think it will be long before our troops are here to take Alaska back," said Collins.

"I sure hope you're right. We need to stay alert and not give the NWA a chance at winning this part of the country back for good," said Jim.

The six-man team left at the crossroads by the road block changed out with fresh militia members from time to time; they had been there for the better part of the summer. Not much had changed; the area was still guarded by nothing but kids, and still no weapons.

They decided to go through the checkpoint and continue north to get more intel.

A four-man team was assembled to go through and see what information they could gather for the mountain residents. Three days passed with no word from the team that went north. A twelve man LRRP was assembled to skirt the road north. Two days after they left, they contacted the mountain by radio on the secure encrypted net.

"Mongoose, this is Diamondback, over."

"This is Mongoose, go ahead."

"We have located the missing team break, they are being detained, break, we can get them with minimal force, over."

"Diamondback, you have a go, break, we are on our way to assist, over."

"Diamondback copies all, out."

The twelve-man team planned to get the detained men out, while a larger force was mobilizing from the cave to meet them on the road, just in case they needed assistance.

As they drove down the road north to meet the two teams, the radio lit up with traffic. There was gunfire and screams.

"Mongoose, this is Diamondback, we are under heavy fire and heading south in a stolen APC. We require assistance, over!"

"Diamondback, this is Mongoose we are passing checkpoint Lima Bravo and heading north over."

Just then, Rick was able to see Jim's convoy coming north toward him.

"Jim, we are almost there, so stop and get ready to unleash hell on our pursuers as soon as you see us."

"Roger that," Jim replied. Rick's APC went through the militia's vehicles and turned around to face north. The men got out and joined the ranks.

"How did you do?" asked Jim.

"We lost one man," said Rick.

"Better than four," said Jim. "Does that thing have any ammo in it?" Jim pointed at the main gun on the APC.

"It sure does," said Rick "And I want you up there Danny!"

"It's locked and loaded," Danny replied.

"Get ready boys, here we go," said Rick.

The road in front of them was full of trucks just cresting the hill.

"Light em up!" yelled Jim.

Automatic fire poured down on the NWA for what seemed like an eternity. Vehicles were riddled with holes and some caught on fire. Very few rounds were fired back before everyone that came toward them was more or less cut down. A few minutes passed.

"Cease fire!" yelled Jim.

The firing stopped from the militia side, but continued sporadically from the other.

"I want only snipers with night vision to engage. Everyone else, heads down," said Jim.

The snipers engaged the enemy for about twenty minutes, until all shooting stopped.

"We will wait here until first light," said Jim. "We will then recover what we can and head home unless we are attacked, and then we will destroy them too."

At first light the main force of militia slowly moved up the road with sniper cover from both flanks. As they moved, the snipers would tell them to stop, a round or two would fire, then they'd get the go ahead to continue.

The men reached the first bullet riddled vehicles and began searching for weapons, ammo and supplies. As they made their way to the last vehicle, they realized that there were no survivors. The final count was forty-seven enemies KIA. The men left the area and headed south to the mountain stronghold, to prepare for the inevitable, the NWA strike back. No one knew for sure if they would come after the militia, but it was better to be prepared.

"You cannot strengthen the weak, by weakening the strong."

—*Abraham Lincoln*

Chapter Twenty-Four: Why we fight

The cave was exploding with questions from all sides. "You all need to calm down!" Jim yelled. "This is what we know. The NWA is back and ready for a fight. The U.S. Military is engaged in the lower forty-eight and we don't know when they will be able to help us. For now, we are on our own and people, we have done pretty damn well so far without them."

Jim said this, but hoped to hell the military would answer their calls for help and get there in time. "We are as well prepared as any military unit can be, and that is what we are," said Jim. "With the machine guns and mortars on our perimeter, we can hold off a very large force. Most of you have more combat experience than many men that I was in the Corps with. I have complete faith in all of you to do your job to defend this community against any size force that comes our way." The crowd yelled and whistled in their agreement with Jim's words.

Everyone dispersed to continue on with their duties.

"Do you really think we have a chance Jim?" asked Matt.

"If it's just troops and APCs that they throw at us, then yes I do. If they have air support and tanks, there is no way in hell we can defend against that," said Jim. "Time will tell, but we have to keep morale up because winter is upon us."

Everyone in the cave was on edge as it grew colder outside. There was talk of surrender if it came to an all out battle. Jim quickly asked everyone to stop talking of defeat, especially when they were so strong.

The first snow came in no time, and they still hadn't had much of a fight out of the NWA. They had ambushed the small contingent the mountain compound had left in town a few times, but didn't get past them.

But on a cold November morning, Bill woke Jim with some disturbing news. The NWA had attacked the outpost in town and almost completely wiped it out. "That was twenty men we had there," said Jim. "Did anyone make it out?"

"We have a few survivors on their way back up here," Bill said. "The initial reports we got on the radio said that they had tanks and hundreds of troops. When the men get back up here, we will know everything."

"I want to take thirty men to meet them on their way up," said Jim. "If they are followed, I want to hit the enemy hard and make them wonder if they should keep coming."

"I'll join you," said Bill.

The perimeter was put on high alert, and everyone woke to man their posts. "We have the fight of our lives headed this way," said Jim. "I want everyone armed and ready. The women and children need to get to the other side of the mountain past the underground river. Take as many supplies as you can and come back for more if you need to. I want every man willing and able to be armed and ready to defend our home." Weapons and ammo were handed out to anyone that would stay and fight.

The small contingent left through the southernmost outpost of the perimeter to find the men from town. They made their way down the mountain using night vision and thermal. Six figures were spotted half way down the mountain by the patrol's point man. Everyone stopped, and a challenge rang out when they got close.

"Sandbag," was called out.

"Dike," was answered back.

"It's them," said Jim.

The men found their way to the patrol and were greeted with open arms.

"Nice to see you boys," said Bill.

"Likewise," said Matt.

"We're you being followed?" asked Jim, looking around.

"I don't think so."

"Don't think so, or know so?"

"Listen, we just got our asses handed to us, I don't think so means no!" Matt was obviously not in a good mood and nobody could blame him. He had lost many good friends.

"Let's get you boys home," said Bill.

Two of the men had superficial bullet wounds that could be patched up in no time and they'd rejoin the ranks. The patrol made its way back to the perimeter and through it with little resistance. Everyone was on edge and trigger happy. A sentry fired at the patrol before all of them were through and hit a man. The sentry was very apologetic and didn't think he should stay at his post.

"What do you want to do with him Jim?" asked Bill.

"Nothing, he was doing his job and he hit his target. It's not his fault he didn't get the word of the patrol coming through." The women and children that had gone to the other side of the mountain were told they could come back for now.

Doc was up all night patching up the wounded. They expected to get word from Jessie or the lower perimeter that they were under attack, but the word never came.

December came and the snow continued to fall. Christmas was in full swing and still no attack. Everyone was in good spirits even though they kept thinking about an impending strike. They couldn't let their guard down, because that is what the enemy wanted.

Did it seem paranoid? Maybe it did, but prepared sounded better.

New Year's Day came and still nothing. They couldn't reach the Marines on the net again. Everyone hated not knowing, but dealt with it.

It was getting colder and colder. The outer perimeter informed the stronghold that their heaters weren't working. They needed to maintain the watch, but couldn't risk the frostbite. The cameras stopped working as the cold snap got worse.

With the outer perimeter unsecured, the enemy had an almost clear shot at the mountain. The traps would only stop the troops for so long and the tanks, if they brought any, would roll right through most of them. The temperature was twenty below and getting colder. An ice fog rolled in and made it harder for the sentries to see anything through their spotting scopes. The middle of January was usually a time when it warmed up a bit, but not this year. Everyone would just have to make do and be ready.

"Incoming!" erupted across the radios early one morning. Mortars began falling and tore up earth all across the mountain.

"Where the hell did they come from?" asked a trembling voice on the radio.

"This is Jim, everyone just get inside and hold your fire. I want all sniper teams in position after the bombardment. They are focusing on the lower part of the mountain. They don't know where we are and I want to keep it that way. Matt, organize the women and smaller children and have them get to the other side of the mountain. Everyone else, to the front of the cave and have all weapons and gear checked by a militia member." This had become very familiar to many of the compound residents. There had been many mock raids and they were ready in no time. More women than Jim wanted were armed and ready to fight.

Sniper teams dispersed around the mountain in defilade. They waited until the mortar bombardment stopped and began to take out the gunners on top of the tanks that could be seen, especially those who looked like leaders in the formations. From Jim's initial assessment, there were hundreds of troops and dozens of tanks. Since there was no communication with the Marines and the outpost in town had been destroyed, they had no prior warning that the tanks were coming. It was extremely cold outside, but the NWA was knocking at the front door and like it or not, they had to answer.

Reports were coming in from different parts of the cave system that the shelling of the mountain had caused parts of the tunnels to collapse. People were trapped in some areas and others had been hurt from falling rocks from above. With such a strong enemy force approaching, the people inside would have to wait until the threat outside was dealt with before they could be rescued.

Militia troops were sent to the lower levels of the perimeter to engage the enemy. They were given instructions to engage and displace very quickly in order for the sniper fire to look like it was coming from them. They made their way back up the mountain under heavy machine gun fire from both sides. The men on top were saving the few mortar rounds they had until the last minute. The smoke from all the rounds being fired, the ice fog and the explosions was making it hard for the militia troops to pick out a target, and they were ordered to only shoot at what they could see. The fog of war, as it was called, could make things very difficult. The tanks could only get part of the way up the mountain, but could provide cover for the NWA troops all the way up. They had to be taken out, but how? Some of the tanks had flipped over after finding a few of the traps, but many were left and kept firing. Rick, Matt and Danny led a small group through the tunnels to the cabin side to flank the advancing troops and hopefully confuse them enough for the mortar crews to zero in on the tanks. It seemed to be working until the tanks re-engaged the mountain. They managed to take out a few of them, but too many were left and it seemed like more were rolling in. Jim had an idea for the snipers to try to get rounds down the main gun tubes of the tanks to disable them. Many rounds were fired at the tubes with none getting in. The snipers were dealing with the fog of war, downhill angles, the cold and the impending night coming upon them. Jim was on his Barrett .50 BMG sniper rifle. He shot six times before getting one down the tube. The tank fired and exploded. Many troops on both sides of the tank that were using it as cover were killed in the process.

"It works!" yelled Jim on the radio. "Focus mortar fire on the tanks, and snipers engage the tubes of the main guns."

Machine gun teams focused on the ground troops and the snipers started shooting the tanks' tubes.

Tanks started exploding all around the lower perimeter. They soon ran out of mortar rounds, but had a surplus of machine gun rounds for the Browning .50 cals, M60s and SAWs. They kept up the suppressive fire sporadically all night with different groups displacing so their mortars couldn't get a fix on anyone. The snipers only took breaks to let their rifles cool off, to displace, or to get more ammo. The battle had lasted for sixteen hours and soon, light could be seen on the horizon. Jessie had tried all night to get ahold of the Marines, but had no luck. She detailed the battle as it continued over the net.

Just after dawn and through a thick fog, everyone could hear what sounded like thunder and yelling. They watched as troops ran up the mountain in the deep snow. Jim gave the order to fire at will at about three hundred yards out. The NWA troops fell as a continuous wall of bullets rained from atop the mountain to the enemy below. Tanks started to fire from below the fog and were hitting close to the mouth of the cave. The troops had been decoys for them to fire on so the tanks could zero in on the militia. They fell back, but the bombardment continued to get closer. Larger explosions could be heard mixed in with the tank shells and soon the tanks stopped firing at them all together.

Jim and a few others went outside to try to get an idea of what was happening. Explosions were rocking the bottom of the mountain. Jim looked up to see a C 130 Specter Gunship orbiting above and firing on the NWA tanks and troops. Everyone could hear the difference in the weapons being fired from the 20 mm cannons to the 40mm auto cannon and of course the 105 mm cannon. The fireworks display on the ground was spectacular. Tracer fire could be seen as it fell to earth. The secondary explosions continued even after the gunship moved on to the next target. No one could help looking down at the bombardment. Unfortunately, a few people got hit by incoming rounds from the NWA below that were still alive. They also saw jets flying low and making strafing runs and dropping bombs on the valley. This was a coordinated attack that they could later thank the U.S. Marines and Jessie for. She had finally gotten through, but no one knew it until later.

At that point, the machine gun teams were ordered to stop firing to conserve the depleting ammo supply. As the militia now had the advantage, snipers were told to find targets and engage. This went on for three days. Everyone was so tired, Matt found one man firing over and over at the same corpse until he ran out of ammo and just kept pulling the trigger. The NWA soldier was pinned up against a tree and did not fall with each round fired at him. The militia soldier was relieved and told to report to Doc to get some sleep under his supervision. The shooting stopped when it got too cold to be outside for more than a few minutes. The men kept watch from inside the cave with thermal and night vision. For more than three weeks, no movement was seen.

The extent of the damage and the loss of life had not yet been accounted for due to the extreme cold and rotation of men guarding the perimeter.

"Matt, I need you to grab Danny and get an accurate count of people we have lost. I also need a weapons and ammo count for another offensive," said Jim.

"I will get right on it after my next shift," said Matt.

"No, I need you to get on that task now. Whoever you plan on relieving will need to pull a double," said Jim.

"Okay, but you won't be happy."

Jim was so tired; he had not realized that Matt was his relief. "I will be fine just go and get it done," said Jim. "And Matt, thanks."

"You got it, brother. As soon as I get the counts, I will be back to relieve you."

The weather slowly warmed up over the next week and the militia was finally able to get out of the compound to find their fallen, and to see what they had done to the enemy. They had started the battle with forty-six men on the lines. Seventeen had been considered MIA until they found them either dead or alive. They had prepared everyone the best they could, but everyone knew that death was a possibility. The men all had water and extra food, but how long could it last?

They had a group of faithful patriots and they gave the enemy hell. As the recovery patrol made its way down the mountain under sniper cover, they started to find people and body parts. Finding everyone was going to be difficult. A few militia members looked in a destroyed bunker that had been used for a mid-mountain observation post. They pulled the wood away and found a body. Then they heard a noise. "I have something," one of the men yelled. Everyone went to help. Under more wood and sandbags, they found three half-dead militia members. Jim radioed for Doc to get down the mountain and requested three stretchers and more men. They encountered more bodies as they went further down. Most were NWA soldiers. As they made their way down the mountain, they found that they had destroyed sixteen tanks and APCs and killed more than three hundred NWA troops. Those were the ones that they could actually count, the damage from the bombs from the planes and the mortars was so extensive. There was no way to tell how many troops were really killed in the offensive. No one would ever find out why so many troops and tanks were sent to this location to fight such a small force.

With the three men that were found alive and the bodies that were recovered, sixteen men had been accounted for. "Thirteen KIA, one MIA and three WIA," said Jim.

"It could have been much worse," said Matt.

"Recover as much ammo as you can," said Rick to the men. "We don't know if we will have to do this again…"

The search continued down the mountain until no more bodies or tanks could be found. "Who is the missing soldier?" Jim asked Matt.

"Roger Man something, I can't pronounce it."

"Does he have any family?"

"It doesn't look like he came with anyone," said Matt.

"Post his name on the big board in the common area so we can see if anyone comes forward," said Jim.

Two weeks passed and still no counter attack. The militia had lost nineteen people, mainly to enemy fire, but some to the extreme cold. They no longer had the security that they had a few months before. Everyone was pulling longer sentry duty to compensate.

Jim was on perimeter security just outside the cave when he heard some crunching snow behind him. "You will have work on your stealth if you want to sneak up on me boy."

"How do you always know when I'm behind you dad?" asked Todd.

"The sound of the crunching snow was the first and then the shadow was second son," said Jim. "The snow should be melting soon and then we can enjoy some warm weather again."

"I can't wait for that," said Todd, "Did we get a mission yet?"

"Here is a list of names," said Jim. "I want you to have them armed and ready to go at the cabin by 1400 hours and no, you aren't on the list. You are ready Todd, but I'm not ready to lose you. Now, off you go."

Todd walked away hanging his head. He wanted to help out more than they would let him.

Jim sat and listened to the silence for a while until he was relieved from his post. As he walked back to the cave, he remembered the men he had lost. *How can anyone live with this,* he wondered.

Just before he made his way into the entrance, Jim stopped to listen. He heard a distant sound. "Quiet! Come here boy," he hissed to a young man passing by. "Do you hear that?"

"Yes sir, it sounds like a helicopter."

"Incoming!" yelled Jim on the radio. People scrambled for cover. The response team met Jim at the entrance.

"What is it sir?" asked a young man.

"There is a helicopter out there," said Jim. "Man the machine guns and get ready for the enemy." The top of the mountain was full of militia in an instant.

"Cease fire," came across the radio. It was Jessie.

"What is it?" asked Rick frantically.

"The Marines are back," she said.

"Do not fire on the helicopter," said Rick.

The helicopter landed at the base of the mountain. Jim and a small militia contingent went down to meet them.

"Captain McGee," said Jim as they walked toward each other. "Where the hell have you been?"

"To hell and back," said the captain.

"I thought you didn't make it when that helicopter got hit last year," said Jim.

"It was a close one," said McGee. The two men shook hands and began to walk up the mountain.

"We have been in several states this year, fighting for our very existence as Americans. It looks like you put up a hell of a fight here."

"We lost many," said Jim. "We also took many. I don't like what we do, but I do it for my family and country."

"I know what you mean," said McGee. "The fight is almost over for most of the world. We have combined forces with China and Russia to fight the NWA. We don't know when it will be over completely, but in the meantime things can start to get back to normal here."

"I will believe it when I see it," said Jim.

"The NWA would have been unstoppable if they had gone from one country to the next," said McGee. "But instead, they tried to take it all at once and showed their arrogance. They had too many people fighting them, too many people that enjoyed their freedom."

"We will make a monument here on this mountain and remember the Americans that gave it all for that very freedom, and our way of life," said Jim.

Chapter Twenty-Five: Reconstruction

Captain McGee was a man of his word. The NWA was nowhere to be found and everything seemed to be getting back to normal. Some people wanted to stay in the safety of the cave compound, but Bill made it clear that it was his property and if things were getting back to normal then everyone needed to go back home and get back to their own lives. It took days, but everyone had made their way back down the mountain. Bill and Terry stayed behind to button everything up. Some would be back from the original group for the annual moose hunt in the fall, but Bill wasn't counting on everyone. They had all gone through hell up there and it would just be a reminder.

Jim and his family went back to their home. After arriving in the now beat up subdivision, they were standing out front and staring at their house. It didn't look the same. The fence was torn down and the shed doors and siding were gone. The cedar siding was torn off and the plastic house wrap was all they could see.

"I guess people needed the wood to keep warm," said Mary.

"I suppose so," said Jim. "Let's go kids. Let's see what's inside now." The family went inside the house to find it gutted. "Looks like we will have to make do and rebuild."

"This isn't cool," said Todd.

"War never is," said Alexis.

"We will do what we always do and make do with what we have." Everyone was given a task to carry out and started to fix the house into something they could live in again.

The Stantons were not the only family that had to rebuild in the community. Some houses had burned down and had to be completely rebuilt, so everyone got together and worked on one house at a time. Tents were erected for the most unfortunate families during the construction. Work went slow because of a lack of wood and other supplies needed. The electricity wasn't working yet, but crews were addressing the issue.

Within a few short weeks, the U.S. Army came to help. They brought the hospital back up to working order and provided supplies that were sorely needed. Food started to show up in the grocery stores and people started to get back to work. The banks in the area that had any money left in their vaults started the local monetary system working again. Things seemed great until a curfew was initiated.

Jim went to the local Army commander to inquire about the curfew. First, he was told to wait and to relinquish his sidearm. He didn't like the fact that he had to give them his .45 and had to wait for three hours. Jim was not happy when he could finally see the commander. "What the hell is going on here?" Jim demanded angrily. "And why did I have to give you my .45?"

"Easy there soldier," said the Army colonel.

"I am no soldier," said Jim. "I am a United States Marine and I demand to know why we have a curfew and why we have to ration food." "I thought supplies were flowing in just fine?"

"I have to tell you Jim..." said the Colonel as he poured a drink and offered one to Jim, which he declined. "This sector has it much better than most. I would really hate to be a civilian in the lower forty-eight."

"What do you mean?" asked Jim. "I thought things were getting better?"

"They are, but not at the pace you and everyone else would like. The world was turned upside down not too long ago and needs to be reset. We are in the process of doing just that."

"So, why the curfew?" asked Jim.

"We have had reports of looting and in some cases, rape and murder. We will be handling the security of this community until things get better and a regular police force can be established," said the colonel. "The use of force will only be used as a last resort. The confiscation of all arms will be the first order of business." Jim couldn't believe his ears. Being the smart man he was, he thanked the colonel for his time and left.

On his way home, Jim stopped by Matt's place and told him to gather the militia discreetly. Something needed to be done about this new occupation before it got out of hand. The thirty or so men that Matt could get together met in an old barn close to most of their homes.

"So what is this I hear about the Army confiscating weapons?" asked Rick.

"I was just told this by the new Army commander," said Jim. "We have fought too hard and lost too much to be tossed from one occupation force to the next. Who is with me?" asked Jim. Everyone stepped forward.

"We need a plan," said Matt.

The men all sat down to figure out what to do.

"How many troops do we have here in town?" asked Jim.

"My wife says about forty," said a man in the back. "She works for the medics down at the hospital."

"Okay, what kinds of weapons are we looking at?" asked Rick.

"I have seen SAWs and .50 cals mounted on the Humvees," said Matt.

"Alright," said Jim, "We need to take out the roving patrols with non-lethal force and roll into the Army compound to show the colonel that we mean business."

In two days, the militia had pinned down the patrol routes of the Army troops and was ready to initiate operation Home Front. The Humvee patrols were stopped with mocked up accidents on the road. As the soldiers got out to assist, they were surrounded by militia. The surprised soldiers quickly gave up and were bound before being taken away. The militia members got in the Humvees and made their way to the compound to show the Colonel what he could expect from the local populace if he continued on down the road he had chosen.

Four Humvees rolled into the old high school that had been turned into an FOB for the Army. Jim fired off a burst from the .50 cal on top the Humvee he was in and the soldiers pointed their weapons at them.

"Tell the colonel we want to talk to him!" yelled Jim.

An Army captain approached the Humvees and demanded to know what they were doing.

"We are United States citizens and demand to be treated with dignity and respect. If it wasn't for us, you would not have the opportunity to be here right now. We have spilled too much blood and lost too many loved ones to be treated like second class citizens. We want common ground and it needs to happen today," said Jim.

The colonel came out of the command trailer and was furious. "What the hell do you think you are doing?" he asked.

"We are here to offer our assistance in rebuilding our community," said Rick. "You want to establish a new police force? Then you need to let us help."

"Like hell I do!" said the colonel.

"Soldiers, take these weapons from these men and place them under arrest." The soldiers moved in and Jim fired another burst into the air.

"Stop now or you will be fired on!" The soldiers looked back at their commander for advice, permission or something.

"We have been fighting in this area for more than three years," said Jim. "And killing has become second nature to us; do you think you will be any different? Put your weapons on the ground slowly and step back," he ordered. The soldiers did as they were told. Most of them looked like kids and not combat veterans.

Jim walked up to the colonel and said, "I think I will be taking my 1911 back now." Jim took it out of the colonel's holster.

"We need a mediator," said Jim, "and I have the perfect one in mind. Colonel, this is Major McGee of First Force Recon USMC." Major McGee stepped out of a Humvee and walked up to the men.

"I will not be taking orders from a major," said the colonel.

"I am not here to make demands, colonel. I have been asked to come here on behalf of the people of this wonderful community. I would not be here today if it wasn't for the gallantry of these very fine men. I fought beside them when they had no hope and were triumphant in the face of certain death. I really think you should listen to what they have to say and take their offer to assist you. They have lived here for a long time. They can and will want to help."

"I will not give up my weapons for any comfort you can offer," said Jim. "I will however, use my weapons to help police this community and bring to justice anyone that threatens its harmony. We are patriots and many are prior military. We were uprooted by an enemy that would have rather seen us gone from this earth. I used to own a gun store and we have a few cops and corrections officers. We can help you if you will listen and let us."

"I have my orders," said the colonel. "I cannot disobey them."

"But you can question them and offer to your commanders our assistance. We do live here," said Matt.

"We know the area and the people," said Jim. "We will not just sit by and let your men do as they want without consequence. Get your commander on the line and let him know we want to help," he continued. "You don't want the alternative. We are tired of fighting, but will continue if we are threatened."

The colonel was reluctant, but made the call. After a few minutes of what seemed like arguing, he got off the phone and told Jim that his help was welcomed.

"Now, where are my men?" asked the colonel.

"Bring them into the compound boys," said Jim over his radio. A school bus rolled in and the soldiers got off. The militia brought in bags full of gun parts, ammo and gear. It was all thrown out onto the ground for them to pick up.

"We will be back here tomorrow," said Matt. The men thanked Major McGee and went on their way back home. The next day, the men that needed work and were qualified for law enforcement showed up to receive their duties.

Chapter Twenty-Six: Life Renewed

"I don't know if I can do this Mary..." said Jim.

"I know you can," she said. "You are the strongest man I know and will do just fine." Jim was appointed sheriff by the local interim government and was in charge of six officers. He and the others were chosen based on recommendations and the fact that most of them had commanded men in battle was a clincher.

"I have always owned my own business, never really liked 'the man,' and now I am 'the man."

"You will do great," said Mary. "Now get to work and bring me home some money!" Mary was laughing and trying to keep Jim's spirits up.

"Okay, I suppose I did bring this on myself," he said.

"You were chosen for a reason. Men followed you into battle and trusted you with their lives. This will be no different except you won't be shot at as much," Mary said, still smiling.

He hugged, kissed and thanked his wife for her support. Jim got in his new patrol car and headed to the station. Most of the local law enforcement had been killed by the invading NWA. The city had to start from scratch in many aspects of the community. One man on the newly formed police force had been an officer before from another town. He would be Jim's right hand man.

"Lance, do you have that roster?" asked Jim.

"Right here sheriff."

"Ok, let's see, um, Smith."

"Here."

"Davis?"

"Here."

"Perry?"

"Here."

"Daniels?"

"Here."

"And Green?"

"Here sir."

"Men, we are the new line of defense for the local population and we will be helpful, courteous and uphold the law. Is that understood?"

"Yes, sir," said the men all together.

"You have your orders, now go out there and show them they can rely on us and remember, the military is there to help only as a last resort. We need to do this on our own. We have not fully recovered so I want you to be very cautious. These people are our neighbors, but they have had it hard and still might resort to violence to get what they want because they have had to for so many years. Just reassure them that you are there to help and call for back up at the slightest sense of problems."

"Perry, in my office," said Jim. Rick entered and closed the door. "Well, is this better than being a mechanic?"

"I will let you know tomorrow," Rick said with a smile. "Thanks for putting in a good word for me, brother."

"I need people on my side I can trust," said Jim. "You better get out there."

Davis was the dispatcher until one could be found to fill his position. He or she would have to be able to handle any situation on the phone and answer questions as they came in.

With a new understanding between the occupying U.S. forces and the people that fought in the area to defend their own land, things were on a fast track to full recovery and life almost looked normal. Local law enforcement was something that everyone knew was needed and there would be problems to be dealt with, but the question was how to deal with them. A new set of laws were implemented after an appointed group of people read through the old ones. Like you found in many places, some of the craziest and absurd laws could be found and taken out and replaced with common sense ones.

Most people had their old jobs back, but for the people that had jobs that didn't matter now, it was back to training in a new field. Construction was one of the main jobs available, even if it wasn't what you wanted you took it to survive in a changed world.

Life seemed easier to most, and could be enjoyed with family and friends. The Internet and TV were not an interruption people had to their daily lives for now. There were many block parties and barbeques that hadn't taken place before. People had time to focus on what really mattered and were happier. Much of the housing was still unoccupied and parts of the city looked like a ghost town. The people of the area had lost so much and it was time to rebuild.

Elections for the local government were a top priority for the U.S. Military in order to get the area infrastructure back up and running. With local officials, their hope was that they could eventually leave and go to another area. It all sounded good, but government is what got them in this mess to begin with. Not many people were looking forward to voting for someone that might be willing to do the job.

Jim put together a town hall meeting to discuss the issue with the locals, but it turned into something much larger. The night of the meeting Jim was again a little nervous to be in front of all the people. Mary reassured him as she always did. They went to the meeting together at the old Sports Center. The meeting was held there in order to get as many people involved as possible. Thousands showed up and the meeting had to be moved outside. After the podium was set up and security was in place, Jim got up to announce the singer of the National Anthem. The singer was his daughter Alexis. Everyone got quiet and she sang her heart out. She surprised everyone by not only singing the first verse, but the second as well.

The crowd exploded in whistles and cheers when she finished. Many people up front were in tears. Jim hugged his little girl and thanked her. The next speaker was a local church pastor. He said a small prayer for the crowd about God, the country and freedom and introduced the temporary local government. Politics were to be run differently from now on. No more political careers, one term was all that was allowed and officials had to hold a day job as well. They got paid the same as anyone else in office, no matter the position. Only the jobs that were needed to govern the people were to be available, no more bloated Government. A citizen legislator was what the founding fathers of the United States wanted, and for good reason. The crowd seemed to agree with this. With the politics concluded, a small carnival was set up for the kids to enjoy.

"We haven't been to one of these in a long time," Mary said to Jim.

"We thought it would bring more people together and make them feel at home in the community," said Jim.

The night ended with fireworks.

The next day around town, the mood was blissful everywhere they went. American flags were flying with pride in more places than anyone had ever seen.

"Mission accomplished," said one of the men running for mayor to some of his supporters that were campaigning outside of the local grocery store.

"What do you mean sir?" asked a woman at the table.

"Look around and see how happy people are. Now hand out those fliers with a smile," he said. "And let's win an election!"

Jim was on patrol one day and got a call from dispatch to go to a local store. He was told that the local merchant called about the military busting up his store. Jim called for two other officers to meet him there. The Humvees were driving away as they approached the store. Jim and the others got out of their patrol cars and went inside to find out what had happened.

"They just came in here and started to take things," said Mack, the owner of the pawn shop. "They started to break things when I didn't have what they wanted and that's when I called you."

"Okay boys," said Jim. "Get your rifles out of your trunks and get your gear on. We are going to have a talk with the military." The men got into their cruisers and sped off toward the Army compound with their lights and sirens on.

"Slow down boys," said Jim as they got close. "And turn off the sirens and lights." They approached the guard shack on the perimeter and had weapons pointed at them. Jim got out of his car and walked up to the shack.

"That's far enough, sir," said an MP as weapons were pointed at him.

"I need to talk to the colonel."

"Not going to happen," said the MP.

"Son, you don't seem to understand," said Jim. We just had some of your troops bust up a local business and we need to get this figured out."

Safeties were clicked off and more soldiers approached the gate. "You need to get back in your car and leave, sir," said the MP.

"I understand," said Jim. "We will be on our way." With that, the police officers all got back into their cars and drove back to the station.

Jim got on the phone and called everyone he knew to bring all their friends with guns and ammo. "We need to put a stop to this, now." About four hundred men showed up at a ranch just outside of town.

"Men!" shouted Jim. "This is the situation. We have about two hundred heavily armed U.S. soldiers that need a helping hand to leave town and I need your help to accomplish this. Some soldiers have been getting out of hand and think they are above the law. We are going to show them otherwise." All of the men geared up and looked as if they were in combat again.

The old school that was now the Army compound, would be surrounded on two sides, with sniper cover enveloping the other two along while providing overwatch for the ground troops.

The men all left for the school in trucks converted to hold machineguns on top that were left over from the occupation of the NWA. Two trucks rolled up to the gate and were considered hostile unless they turned around, so a sign said. Jim got out and yelled "Surrender!"

The soldiers laughed.

"Hit it!" Jim said over the radio, and militia came out of the woods to surround the compound. The soldiers stopped laughing, as they could see they were surrounded and outnumbered. "Lay down your weapons and surrender. This is your last warning," said Jim. Soldiers started to lay their rifles down. "We have heavy machine guns and snipers all around your perimeter, now all of you lay down your rifles." The militia entered the compound and disarmed the rest of the soldiers. They were loaded onto their own trucks and escorted out of town without their weapons.

"We will have these sent to you in Anchorage," said Rick to the colonel before he left.

A road block was established about fifteen miles north of town in order to get advanced warning of the Army coming back. It was fortified with sand bags, massive blocks of concrete and light and heavy machine guns from .50 cal on down to 5.56mm.

Jim got in contact with Major McGee as soon as he got back to town to let him know what they had to do. He wasn't surprised. "With martial law in effect, the U.S. troops are almost as bad as the invading armies were," said McGee. He agreed to get word to the regional Army commander that the people no longer needed troops on the Southern Peninsula.

The elections went well and they had a new mayor and city council. The other close towns were doing the same thing in order to bring their towns back to life. For now, they just got air drops from the Air Force to supplement the supplies they couldn't get or grow until the airports could be repaired. The area was a model for others to use to get back to normal.

In a short time, they were able to remove the road block and store all the military gear and weapons in the old armory. Instead of having a local Army National Guard, they had their own militia get together one weekend a month and two weeks a year. The participation was great, with hundreds of members and real uniforms, ranks and jobs. They had a combat force ready to defend the community at a moment's notice. It was mentioned that this size force would have been nice to defend against the NWA when they were here, but they did just fine back then as a guerilla force.

The men came up with the name Phoenix Group for the local militia because they had risen from the ashes and were ready to unleash hell on all enemies foreign and domestic. Flags were made with fire and the phoenix upon them.

Every year there was a parade and celebration to commemorate the end of a long, cold and bloody war. On that day, everyone that had fought at Freedom Mountain as it was now called made their way to it to visit the memorial that was built next to the cemetery for the fallen of World War III.

Once again, as Americans, the people had won their freedom back from the oppression of a foreign enemy. The country slowly transformed back into the real America there had once been. Life on the streets and around the town was like a movie out of the 1950s. People actually cared for one another again.

The world was changed, however. Borders that used to be between two or three countries no longer existed. There were now larger countries to contend with. Most of Europe was one country now, so was most of Africa. Where the One World Power failed, others prevailed. The earth no longer had hundreds of countries, but dozens. The United States was still a major power in the grand scheme of things. All the troops that they used to have in so many countries were now guarding this one. The way things should be.

"A well-regulated Militia, being necessary to the security of a Free State, the right of the people to keep and bear Arms, shall not be infringed."

2nd Amendment
December 15th 1791

Special thanks to:

Eric Cox
Matt Cook
T.J. Cox
Craig Dixon
Logan Parks
Melanie Noblin (for help with the cover)
Hannah Heimbuch (for putting up with me)

Made in the USA
San Bernardino, CA
07 April 2013